A NORFOLK MAN

Jeremy Cameron

Majolier Press

ISBN-13:

978-1-7392324-2-9 (Paperback)

978-1-7392324-3-6 (Ebook)

Book cover and formatting by Katie Mackenzie

First edition 2024

FOREWORD

A Norfolk Man is the novel that Jeremy Cameron was working on at the time of his death. He was keen to see it published.

Jeremy had been working on this book for some time, and although he didn't tell us if it was ready for publication, he had approached publishers and I believe this version was very close to being the final draft. An editor friend had sent some minor suggestions shortly before Jeremy's death, but we don't know what he thought about them.

This was Jeremy's final work and it held significant meaning for him. I have therefore opted to publish it exactly as he left it.

Katie Mackenzie

(Jeremy Cameron's niece)

April 2024

ONE

High above the tractor, a thousand starlings swooped, twisted and rose again, all together, all synchronised as if they were magnetic. How did they all turn at the same time? How did they all know what the others would do? Nicholas watched them as they disappeared over the edge of the field.

"Oy! Young Nick! You woolgathering or what?"

"Sorry! Sorry, Bill." The clutch pedal was so stiff that he had to stand on it to push it down and bring the tractor to a halt. He lifted his foot but he was not strong enough to do it slowly. The tractor and trailer jolted forward.

"Whoa there!"

"Sorry, Bill. Sorry, Ernie. Sorry, John."

They all laughed. The throttle was set so low that the tractor, having jolted once, now crept forward at a snail's pace. Bill and Ernie walked beside it, lifting straw bales on to the trailer with pitchforks. John stacked them on the trailer. Each time they reached a heap of bales they shouted "whoa" to Nicholas and he stopped the tractor. Then they shouted "giddup" to start him again. All three men had grown up working with horses. John, the oldest of them, cursed the tractor as he had cursed the horses. It was not aimed at Nicholas. It was the beast that he didn't care for.

The sun began to penetrate the morning mist. Still too wet to cut corn, they went straw carting after breakfast. Breakfast was from 8.40 until 9.00. By ten o'clock the day was hot.

In the school holidays Nicholas always went round the farm after breakfast. If the men were working in the fields he messed about in the sheds, looking at the cattle or climbing on the combine or binder or thrasher. If the men were still in the yard he asked if he could go to work with them. If it was raining they found work indoors. Sometimes they would play cricket with him.

Today they were taking the four-wheel trailer out of the shed, which had to mean straw carting.

"Bill! Bill! Can I come?"

"Ask your mum."

"She'll say yes."

"Ask her anyhow. And tell her you want some dinner. And a drink."

Nicholas hared back to the house and flung open the back door. His mother was starting the washing, putting towels into a boiler.

"Mum! Bill says I want some dinner and a drink!"

"Does he now? Why does he say that?"

"They're letting me go with them."

"Not combining. You can't go in the harvest field on your own."

"Straw carting. They're going straw carting. All of them. Bill, Ernie, John-boy."

"Just John, I think, to you, not John-boy. All right, hang on, let's get you a drink. I'll bring you some lunch later. What field are they on?"

"Er.... They were cutting on The Git yesterday. No, they were baling on the Thirty Acres before that. And they were baling on the Old Wood before that."

She laughed. "In fact you don't know. Just a minute, let me come down to the yard with you." She found his school satchel and an old Corona bottle, tipped some orange squash in the bottle and filled it with water. Then she took off her apron, dabbed at her hair and changed her shoes. All the while Nicholas stood at the open door, shifting from foot to foot.

They left the house together and Nicholas ran back to the yard, his mother walking behind. She smiled at the men, waiting in the yard, Bill on the tractor, Ernie and John sitting on a straw bale on the trailer.

"Morning, Mrs Hutton."

"Morning, Bill. Ernie. John. It's very nice of you to take Nicholas. Where are you going?"

"The Old Wood. That all right with you?"

"Fine. Don't let him get in your way. Send him home any time."

"Won't be in the way. Set him to work. Drive the tractor a bit."

"Are you sure? He won't be a nuisance?"

3

"Only three of us. Two pitchers and a loader. Need the help. Ought to be paying him."

They all laughed.

"I'll bring his lunch up later. Will you be combining this afternoon?"

"More than likely."

She waved and went off. Nicholas climbed on the drawbar of the tractor and round the front sail of the trailer. Squeezing past, one of the men grabbed his arm until he was safely on the trailer floor. He sat on a bale with John.

"How's your off cutter then, young Nick? You been practising?"

John was in his mid-sixties and no longer nimble. However, he claimed that his off cutter was a piece of magic that had mystified the greatest batsmen in Norfolk. It was before the war. In fact it was before the first war. Welbeck had two cricket teams then and they played all the surrounding villages. When they couldn't walk to matches they cycled. Later, they sometimes hired a charabanc. John had been, according to him, the terror of nine parishes. Nowadays in the farmyard he had a slow walk to the wicket and a low trajectory, but on the dirt and stones in front of the barn door he could still be unplayable.

"I can't get it to go like yours, John. I can't get the right spit on the ball."

"Oo-ah. The right spit."

John and Ernie were shaking their heads slightly.

"Well, let me think now." John said. "Maybe you ask your mum for some special food. Get some spit in you."

"Couple of pints of brown and mild every night," Ernie suggested. "Give John that spit."

"My mum likes a glass of sherry sometimes."

"Glass of sherry. Hmmm. Got to look that one up, I reckon."

"In the instruction book."

The two men looked down at their feet

"Glass of sherry, John."

"Try that one day."

In the field now, they moved to the next heap of bales. Nicholas stood on the clutch again and the tractor rolled to a halt. Thirty yards away a rabbit was grazing, ignoring them. Bill came round the side of the tractor and reached beside the seat. On the floor was his catapult. He took it out quietly, found a large stone, fitted it into the elastic and took aim. Half a second later the rabbit squirmed in agony. Bill ran over and killed it.

Unfortunately the excitement was too much for Nicholas, whose foot slipped again off the clutch pedal. The tractor jolted forward and John fell over on the trailer. His cry of anger split the field.

"Sorry!" Nicholas cried. "Sorry, John!"

"Bloody tractor. Bloody wars. Bloody machine. The hell if I know."

Bill came back with the rabbit, which he laid with the catapult on the floor of the tractor. "Tea tomorrow," he announced. "If we get another one you can have it for your mum."

"Thanks, Bill."

"Now you keep that tractor rolling, eh?"

"I'm sorry John fell over again."

"Don't you worry about him. He's used to it."

The tractor had no cab and was open to all weathers; in the rain the men wore a waterproof cape, in the winter they wrapped themselves in layers of clothing. Nicholas could clamber up and down on the tractor, indeed had been doing so for three or four years. Now, with the end of his foot he could touch the poor dead rabbit if he chose. At the moment, however, both feet were required for the clutch pedal and so was all his concentration.

Just before twelve, when in truth he was exhausted, his mother arrived with a package of sandwiches wrapped in newspaper and another bottle of squash. She walked across the field swinging the shopping bag she was carrying them in.

"There's your mum."

"Right on time. Thought for a minute you was going to eat my dinner."

Bill stopped the tractor and Nicholas climbed down. The men walked across to the stack they were building in the corner of the field. They arranged a few bales against the stack and made themselves comfortable.

"Mrs Hutton."

"Hello, men. Has he been behaving himself?"

"Won't let us stop, Mrs H. Slave driver. We keep begging for a rest, he tells us we got to carry on."

"It isn't true! And by the way, Mum, Bill shot a rabbit with his catapult!"

"Did he really? Well done, Bill."

"We'll be getting the combine out after dinner. He can drive that too if he wants."

"Can I?!"

"Certainly not, Nicholas. They're just teasing you. You can have your lunch with the men, then come home. You're not to go in the harvest field."

She turned to the men. "Thanks very much indeed, chaps. He'll probably be pestering you again tomorrow."

"Quite all right, Mrs Hutton. He hin't been no trouble."

She went off home, still swinging the empty bag, and Nicholas turned to his food.

"Good grub by the look of it."

"Better than John's anyhow I dare say."

"Watch him now."

John picked at his sandwiches, pulled them around and threw most of them into the field for the birds.

"Always throws them away. One day when he weren't looking we put them back in his bag. His missis found them later. Didn't he get wrong!"

John threw them a dark look but said nothing.

"He don't eat no food. Brown and mild keeps him going. In't that right, John?"

"Never you mind."

"Falls off his bike every night coming home from the Crown, picks himself up again. Sometimes falls off again coming to work in the morning. Still drunk." Bill and Ernie laughed.

John threw a sandwich at them. They laughed again.

"Policeman stopped him one night. No lights on his bike. Weren't worried about him falling off, only him having no lights. You weren't frit of no policeman though, John, were you?"

John said nothing.

"Asked the policeman to walk in front of him holding his torch!"

They all looked down at their food.

Nicholas trudged home across the yard. The men came back to collect the combine and the sacks to shoot the corn in, before going off to the barley field. Nicholas realised that he could have had his dinner at home but his mother had let him eat with the men. As he came in the back door she was finishing her own sandwich, drinking a cup of coffee.

"Hello, dear. Had a good morning?"

"Mum, we carted five acres. It weren't very thick, mind."

"It weren't very thick?"

"Er, it wasn't very thick."

"Mind?"

"Well, that's what they say, Mum!"

She smiled. "I don't think they'll talk like that when you go away to school. Now, what are you going to do this afternoon? First I think you should have a rest."

"Can I have a sweet?"

"Go on. You know where they are. Only two a day though."

He went upstairs for his rest and read his favourite book, which he had already read five times, Gimlet, King of the Commandos.

"Bypass the pillbox!" Whatever could it mean? It was the sort of language that Gimlet used, and, as it was his favourite book, Nicholas was reluctant to admit that he didn't understand it. What was bypass? What was a pillbox? Was it a box with pills in it? He went back to the bit where Trapper steals up to a German and cuts his throat. He could understand that better. Listening to his mother moving around downstairs and the combine leaving the yard, he burrowed into his book.

"Terry's here! Nicholas! Terry's here!"

Nicholas woke on hearing his mother's voice, struggled from his bed and came slowly downstairs rubbing his eyes. "Hello, Terry," he said.

"Was you sleeping?"

"I think so. I was having my rest."

"My gran reckons all that resting makes you die young. She goes how you spend long enough dead, you got to make the most of your time alive."

"Your gran talks a lot of old squit."

Terry laughed at that and they went outside. "Race you to the shed."

They tore across the farmyard, still muddy even in August, and ran into the feed shed. At this time of year the sheds were empty of cattle during the day. The cows came in at night but the bullocks stayed in the field. The boys jumped on to the feed sacks and climbed higher until they could reach the ceiling. They turned round and sat on the sacks.

"What did you do this morning?" Nicholas asked.

"Helped my mum. Did the garden. You know. Me and my sister. Only she can't dig."

"I was straw carting."

"Lucky so-and-so."

"We carted five acres."

"You think I can go straw carting?"

"Yeah. I'll ask Bill."

"You call him Bill? Not Mr Spooner?"

"I always call him Bill. Mum calls him Bill."

"What does he call her?"

"He calls her Mrs Hutton."

They thought about this. "Tha's a rum job," Terry said eventually.

They spent the afternoon playing on the cattle feed and out the back of the sheds. They talked about cricket. England were playing Australia at the Oval, though that was almost all they knew. As they crossed the yard for a drink, two planes flew overhead.

"Spitfire!" exclaimed Nicholas. "Spitfire!"

"It's a Hurricane!"

Nicholas was prepared to bow to superior knowledge. His mother had smilingly told him that he didn't know a Spitfire from a cricket bat. All the same, he wished it was a Spitfire.

"I'm going away to school soon," he said as they went through the door.

"What?"

"I'm going away to boarding school."

"Boarding school? What's that?"

"Where you stay. Don't come home."

"Don't come home? For ever?"

"No, stupid. Come home for holidays."

Terry was completely nonplussed. "You stay at school at night?" He was trying to imagine staying at school at night. "What about your tea? When do you get your tea?"

"You get your tea at school. Like your dinner. I suppose."

"What about feeding the chickens? Taking the dog out?"

"Someone else has to do it. Your mum."

"My mum never feeds the chickens."

"Some boys got dads. Maybe they do it."

JEREMY CAMERON

They went in the kitchen, where Nicholas' mother was drinking a cup of tea and smoking a cigarette. "Hello, boys," she said. "Hungry, thirsty or both?"

"Mostly thirsty."

"Mrs Hutton... ?"

"Yes, Terry?"

"That right, Nick's going away to school?"

"Yes, Terry. Next term he's going away to school."

"Why?"

"Why?" She paused while she got out the orange squash. "Why? Well, I think it will help him with his school work, I suppose."

"He don't come home at night?"

"Not in the term time, no."

"Blimey."

"Do I have to?" Nicholas asked suddenly.

"Well, dear, I think it's best."

"All right."

They drank their drinks and went out again. John-boy was in the farmyard, leading in half a dozen cows from the field. The cows needed no direction but made their own way into the shed to be milked, each one taking up a milking station. John had to be spared from the harvest field to get them in.

"Can we do the milking?" Nicholas asked.

"You done the rest today, driv the tractor, carted straw. Best you do the milking too, I reckon."

"Thanks, John."

John led them inside, put clean buckets under the cows, placed a stool beside the first one and cleaned her udders. Nicholas sat on the stool and placed his hands tentatively round the cow's teats.

"Do it like you mean it, lad. Grab hold of her proper."

Nicholas squeezed and pulled on the cow's teats while she ate from the manger in front of her. Milk came in satisfying squirts as he pulled more vigorously. John set Terry up with the next cow then went to the third himself. A satisfied silence fell over the cows and the milkers, Nicholas and Terry concentrating, determined to miss nothing. After a while John came round and gave a good pull on each teat to make sure the cow was empty, then set the boys up with their next two. When they had finished he gave them each some milk in a bottle to take home, then tipped the rest into a churn for collection.

It was time for tea. Nicholas ran across the farmyard, though more slowly than he had gone in the opposite direction. Terry went home to feed the chickens and have his own tea.

The day was cooling now. In the background Nicholas could hear the distant hum of the combine, which would keep going until the dew forced a halt. He liked teatime, when his mother asked him about his day at school or on the farm. He saved up things throughout the day to tell her.

Two

Dear Frances,

I have just put Nicholas to bed and I can relax with a glass of sherry and write to you at my leisure. It is a glorious evening. The sun went down in a crimson haze and the men on the farm have just finished harvesting for the day. They haven't brought the combine back to the sheds which means that they mustn't have finished a field, so Nicholas tells me. They all came back on the tractor and trailer. Nicholas helped them cart straw this morning - he drove the tractor! They are very good with him and he adores them.

These are the times, I suppose, when I miss Hugh most. Perhaps it is merely selfish. Perhaps it is a delusion: after all, we were barely married when he went away and after that we only had a short time together when he was on leave. Really we barely knew each other. But oh, yes, I do miss him. I would like to sit here in the evening, talk about Nicholas and, well, just sit.

Do you remember, when we were all at home, how we used to sit outside on an evening like this? Reading our books or playing games? Sometimes you and I would sleep in the tent or even just on the grass when it was very hot? Of course we never thought we would grow older but it did seem then as if time stood still. One day just led to another.

Speaking of books, I have discovered a marvellous new author called Angus Wilson. You really must read his short stories. He's very modern and writes about people like us, I think, very wittily. I will lend you one of his books when you next come to stay. William Cooper writes well about this sort of world too, and John Wain, but you know about them already.

Nicholas goes away to school next month; fortunately the money which Hugh put away will cover that. I think it's the right thing to do, sending him away. He's eight now. But it will be very hard for both of us.

I don't really know what I shall do with myself when he is away but this may be the chance I have been waiting for to get back on the stage. Donald Wolfit has written to me several times to ask if I am available for any productions by his company and young Peter Brook, whom I don't know, made contact once because he saw me when he was a boy - in one of Noel's plays, I think - and he asked if I was interested in the right part. It's very flattering but I'm so out of practice that I don't know what I'd be like. I'd probably play Beatrice with a Norfolk accent! "Cor, tha's a rum old job, Benedick bor! That'll larn yer!"

It's been so long since I did anything, really, except look after Nicholas. A week or two ago I went to a lunchtime concert in King's Lynn while Nicholas was at school. This is what passes for excitement in my life now. It was a harpist.... He was very good but frankly it was rather boring. Anyway, after it was all over I was having a cup of tea in the restaurant they have got there and this man came up, very smart, quite good looking, married I suppose, and asked if he could join me. We chatted for a few minutes about music, and books, and the weather, that sort of thing - I don't think he knew who I was, either that I was a widow or that I used to act - and I could swear he was about to ask me to dinner or something. Then I think he saw the look of abject terror on my face and he swallowed it up, whatever proposal it was, and soon fled.

It has been so long, Frances, since I was alone with a man! I, who, I may say in all modesty, had a fair number of proposals of all sorts in the old days. Yes, I know there was that brief thing with Bertie Wilson not long after Hugh died, but that wasn't real, it was just on the backlash and it was all over in a few weeks. It was so difficult to get anyone to look after Nicholas - and I felt so guilty! But I can't go on like the ice queen. I don't think I'm pushing Nicholas away to school, because he was bound to go anyway. But if I could do some acting, and have some personal life, well...

Incidentally the money would be handy too, but I've got enough to manage.

Darling, I have gone on for far too long, but I just wanted to write to you and then I got a bit carried away. I don't usually feel so sorry for myself. It is such a lovely place to live and the people are so kind to both of us. I'm just a bit bored, I suppose, that's all.

Are you coming to stay again soon? That would be lovely. Or should we come down to see you before school starts? If I can tear Nicholas away from the harvest, that is.

With all my love,

Helena

THREE

The Goodbodys, Mr and Mrs, lived at the other end of the village. Until recently, Mr Goodbody had been the head gamekeeper. Five gamekeepers worked on the estate and he bicycled between them each day, giving them their instructions, and bicycled an extra time on Fridays to distribute their wage packets. Regular as clockwork, when Nicholas was walking home from school on Fridays Mr Goodbody would cycle past and exchange greetings.

On his retirement earlier in the year, a collection was taken on the estate to buy him a television to watch the Coronation. It was the first television in the village; electricity had arrived only a couple of years earlier. On the day of the Coronation the home of the Goodbodys was packed. Nicholas sat on the floor; his mother was found a chair. Everyone brought buns and drinks and the whole village, or as many as could be packed in, watched the ceremony as it flickered in black and white, sometimes disappearing altogether, in the corner of the couple's small front room. The star of the Coronation was the queen of Tonga, resplendent in the traditional dress of her country, full of colours that could only be described by the commentators.

Afterwards Nicholas could not remember a great deal of the proceedings, but he did remember a discussion about when the queen would have a break to go to the lavatory. "That poor young girl, she must be bursting. And all them clothes to take off and that crown an' all. My Dylis now, she..."

"We don't want to know about your Dylis, Mary. And what's her crown go to do with it? She in't going to pee in that, is she? Not unless she get desperate."

"They don't get desperate like us. They get special training. Hold it in."

"Don't talk a lot of squit, Mary. Look, they just stopped for elevenses. They'll help her with all them clothes."

"I bet that queen of Tonga, she could go for ever."

When he left that day, Mr Goodbody made it clear to him that he must come round any time he felt like it to see them; he only had to knock on the door, they said, and he was always welcome.

At weekends or after school that summer he sometimes walked down the village to their cottage behind the church. Mrs Goodbody would bring him a drink and a flapjack and he sat in one of their armchairs. Mr Goodbody would ask him about school and then tell him about the time when he started work, over fifty years earlier, just after Queen Victoria died and King Edward came to the throne. He had to walk four miles in the dark to work and four miles home again. Every time Nicholas called, Mr Goodbody told him the same stories until his exasperated wife would cry "Body! You told him that before!"

Mr Goodbody would acknowledge his wife's point but carry on regardless. "He don't mind," he would say, and it was true.

The day after his straw carting, Nicholas hoped to catch the men in the yard again and be offered more work. However, the corn was dry and they were combining straight away. He came back indoors, where his mother was reading the paper and drinking a cup of tea.

"It says here that England might win the test match," she said.

"What, England and Australia?"

Nicholas loved his cricket at school and in the farmyard but had little real idea of international matches.

"Yes, England are playing Australia at The Oval. You ought to go and ask Mr Goodbody if you can watch it on his television."

So it was that he sat in the Goodbodys' front room eating a jam tart and drinking homemade blackcurrant juice as the screen flickered on and off again, went fuzzy and then cleared.

"We've got a good chance today," Mr Goodbody said. "In fact, lad, I don't want to get too excited yet but I think we're going to win."

Nicholas could not imagine Mr Goodbody getting too excited.

"Have we ever beaten Australia before?" he asked.

"Have we? I'll say so. In fact it was just like this in '26, when we beat them for the first time after the Great War. At The Oval, like this time. Jack Hobbs and Wilfred Rhodes did for them, and Maurice Tate. Then we beat them in '32-'33, bodyline, but the less said about that the better. Then we won the last test in '38 when young Len Hutton got 364. Same name as you and your mum, Hutton. After this war, though, Bradman beat us again, then Hassett. This is our first good chance."

"Who's that batting now?"

"That's Denis Compton. Greatest batsman there's ever been. I saw him play in '47. We stayed with my sister in Enfield for our holidays. I went to Lord's. Sun shone all week. Denis got a hundred. And you see that chap at the other end? That's Bill Edrich. Comes from Norfolk. And all his brothers and cousins, they can turn out a full side. My boy Charlie he played against Edrich once. They wanted a couple of fielders for a match at one of them big houses, back in '34 I'm thinking, so they rang up the Colonel and he sent Charlie and young Harry Smith. Got them off work for the day. Edrich, he was only a young boy then, he got fifty."

"Gosh. That must have been good."

"Charlie could tell you all about it. Then Harry Smith got killed in the war. In Africa."

"Oh."

They watched as Compton and Edrich brought the Australian total closer.

"Tell me about when you started work, Mr Goodbody. About how you went out in the dark."

"Oh, them were the days all right. Not the good old days, though. I used to get up at five, my poor old mum made me some porridge and tea and I set off walking. Four miles it were, and we never had tarmac roads in them days. Started work at seven, I was working in the woods then. Dark as hell in winter. Did a day's work then walked home again. In the dark again, like as not. Bed by eight o'clock. Times was hard, young Nicholas. Times was hard."

"Did you go to the war, Mr Goodbody?"

"Ah, yes, I went to the war. The Great War."

"Did you fight the Germans?"

"It's best we don't talk about all that, lad. There's been enough fighting. Look at that! Denis hit a four - we're nearly there! Mother!"

Mrs Goodbody came bustling in. "What's up?"

"We're going to win! We're going to beat them Australians! Look!"

Then England won. Pandemonium broke out in the household. Mr Goodbody stood up, sat down again, bit his pipe and beamed. Mrs Goodbody said "Well I never" several times. Nicholas clapped. England had won the Ashes. It was a day none of them would ever forget. It was better than the Coronation.

"Mum."

"Yes, dear?"

"Tell me about the time you met Dad."

"Again, dear?"

"Yes, Mum. And how you came to live here."

Helena put down her book and sipped her glass of sherry. "The long version or the short version?"

"The long one."

"All right, Nicholas. But I've got to look at the stew in a bit. That saucepan always seems to stick if I'm not careful."

They sat in the conservatory, where the door to the garden was open. Facing west, they had to shield their eyes against the sun. At six o'clock it was still bright, but sometimes Helena told stories in here after supper while the sun went down. Earlier on, she brought the wireless in and they listened to Children's Hour. In winter they sat in the drawing room and listened to the comedies after their meal. Gradually Nicholas would become sleepier until he stumbled upstairs to bed.

"Right from the start, Mum."

"Well, then. Right from the start. I was acting in a play in Liverpool."

"What was it called?"

"Well, it was Shakespeare. As You Like It. I was there in Mr Wolfit's company. He has his own theatre company and I worked for him quite a bit. Well, we were doing the play in Liverpool for a week and it was going quite well; the local papers had all given us good write-ups and I had my picture in the paper. It was about a year after the beginning of the war. When the war first started they thought everything should be shut down. Then they realised people still had to go out and do things, and anyway they needed to be entertained, it was good for the war effort. It was a bad time, it was after Dunkirk and there were air raids on Liverpool as well as London. So, anyway, we were putting on the play."

"Were you the star?"

"I was the leading lady, if you like. It's not quite the same as being a leading lady in London but we did most of the provinces and I got some attention, yes."

"Was that why Dad came to see you?"

"I don't know about that. We were invited on his ship first. He had joined the Fleet Air Arm, that's like the navy's air force, but they all still had a ship they were stationed on. They were berthed in Liverpool for three nights, on their way from Scapa Flow to Gibraltar."

"What was the ship called?"

"It was called The Magnificent. It was huge. It couldn't get right into the harbour at Liverpool so it had to stay outside and they came in on smaller boats."

"What sort of plane did he fly?"

"I don't know, I'm afraid. But fairly soon after that he became a senior officer and he didn't fly as many planes himself. He was too important."

"So did you go out to the ship?"

"We were invited out there, the whole company, on the first day they were there. We went out in a boat called a cutter and we went up on to his ship."

"Was he waiting to meet you?"

"They all were. The ship's captain came first and he introduced us to all the officers. "This is Mr Hutton," he said, and I saw this tall, handsome officer with fair hair and a twinkle in his blue eyes. I fell in love with him there and then."

"Did he have his uniform on?"

"Of course he did, dear. And he looked wonderful in it. He made for me straight away and then he showed me round the ship. Or boat as he called it. Just me he showed round. He sort of separated me from the others. I heard the rest of the officers laughing but he didn't care. He just swept me off my feet."

"What was the ship like?"

"Oh, you're so romantic, Nicholas, all you want to know is about the ship. Well, it was very big, I can tell you that. All I wanted was to look at Mr Hutton, though. Mr Hugh Hutton, he told me straight away. His friends often called him HH."

"Did he come and watch the play?"

"That night most of the officers came. Afterwards he came backstage and then he took me out for supper. It was quite a short one because he had to be back on the ship. The next day he managed to scrounge a day off. And somehow he scrounged a car and some petrol. We drove up to Southport and walked along the beach and went on the pier. Then he came to the play again and we went out to supper, then he had to go back to the ship again. The next day they were gone."

"Gone? Where did they go?"

"They went to Gibraltar. They were patrolling the Mediterranean. He wrote to me and then we spent a week together when he was on leave."

"Did you? Where did you go?"

"First we went to his parents' house in Norfolk, your granny and granddad Hutton. I was working in London. Then I took him to meet my family, your granny and granddad Manning. Then we had a weekend on our own without anyone. That was a secret."

"A secret? Why was it a secret?"

"Well, we pretended we were married, you see. We went to a hotel in Brighton for the weekend. Everyone thought he had gone back to his ship but really he was in Brighton with me. Then, the next time he came home on leave, we spent the whole week alone together. The time after that, we got married!"

"Gosh!"

"It was what they call a whirlwind romance. But we were very happy. Dad found us our house here because no-one was living in it and Colonel Spencer, whom he knew, wanted to rent it. And we've been here ever since. Daddy came here when he was on leave. Then of course he got sent to the Far East after the war in Europe was over."

"What happened then?"

"He was killed, darling, as you know. The Japanese bombed his ship and a lot of people were killed including your father. So we shall never see him again."

"How old was I when he was killed?"

"You were just six months old, darling. He saw you when you were born, then two weeks later he went to the Far East."

For a moment Nicholas thought his mother was crying, but it was an illusion.

A few days later, just as they were finishing breakfast, Bill knocked on the back door, which was open.

"Come in, Bill. Have a cup of tea."

"I won't come in, thank you, Mrs Hutton, having my boots on." He shifted from one foot to the other, waiting for the right moment to say what he wanted to say. "We were only wondering, Lily and me, if we could, that is if he'd like, if Nicholas wanted to come out with us one Sunday. Or Saturday when we're not working." He gathered his thoughts again, trying to contain his own enthusiasm. "Take him down the seaside maybe. Up Hunstanton. Or Castle Rising, see the castle. If he wants to, that is."

"Yeah! Yeah, Mum!"

Helena smiled. "I think you've got your answer there, Bill. I think that would be lovely. It would give me a bit of time to myself as well. I might even go out to lunch with a friend. I'll see. Anyway, I think Nicholas would be very grateful, wouldn't you Nicholas, and so would I. Just you and Lily and him, you wouldn't get fed up with him?"

"We'd lock him in the castle if we got fed up with him, Mrs H. In them dungeons. What they're for, small boys."

"That'd be fine. Give him bread and water."

Nicholas was nearly beside himself. "This Sunday!"

"Well, maybe. If the weather holds and we can go combining all week. Take the day off Sunday then. Feed the cattle, get John-boy to do the milking, leave about ten, take a picnic, come back in time for your tea if that'd suit?"

"That would suit very, very nicely, Bill. Let me make the picnic, though."

"Not at all. Lily, she makes a rare picnic."

"Well, thank you very much."

On the Sunday, Nicholas was out of bed at seven. Helena slept for a few minutes longer until his clattering proved impossible to ignore. She came downstairs in her dressing gown to find him getting his own cornflakes, ready for an early departure.

"Good morning, Nicholas."

"Good morning, Mum." He thought it likely that he was doing something he shouldn't. "Am I going to get wrong?"

"No, you're not going to "get wrong". You're doing very well. It's a bit early, that's all."

"Bill might be here soon."

"He might, but I doubt it. He's got to get his breakfast too, you know. And feed the cattle. And Lily has to make the picnic. All that sort of thing."

She made herself a cup of coffee and lit a cigarette. It was too early for the Sunday paper so she watched as Nicholas' cornflakes disappeared. No sooner had he finished them but a knock came at the door.

"He's here!"

"Already? Go and see if it's him."

The door opened - it was never locked - and Bill poked his head round it. "Can I come in?"

"Just in time for coffee. Or tea. You must have made an early start, Bill. Come on in."

"We.... had a bit of news during the night. But nothing to stop us today. We're all set. I've been over the motor. All looking good. No, I won't have a cup, thanks. I did the cattle so we can start whenever you like."

"Something wrong, Bill?" He had dark marks under his eyes; and his hair, usually immaculate with Brylcreem, was uncombed.

"Nothing to worry the boy about, Mrs Hutton. We're set for a fine day and we mean to enjoy it. What time would you like him back? About teatime?"

"That would be lovely."

Nicholas had already gathered his bag, with some sweets, a drink, a book and his corduroy jacket in it. He ran out of the door, crying "See you later, Mum."

"Have a lovely time, dear. Don't forget your sword!"

Nicholas had a second breakfast with Bill and Lily: fried egg with fried bread. They lived half a mile from the farm; the landowner allocated his houses in parallel order of size and social hierarchy, so Helena had the larger home. They walked across to Bill and Lily's house, gulped down some breakfast and set out.

Bill's car was an old green Austin. He and Helena owned the only cars in the village; hers was unreliable, his was not reliable at all.

They set off first for Heacham, on the coast, and on the way passed through Sandringham where the queen lived. A year earlier Nicholas had seen old Queen Mary there, grandmother of the new queen, starched and stately, waving to the crowds as she passed to church. Today, though, all was quiet. They looked back at the big house as they moved down the avenue towards the coast. As they turned the corner and looked ahead, the country fell away through the flat lands to the sea.

"Can you smell the sea, boy?"

"Can I smell it?"

"You can always smell the sea here. Smell the salt?"

"Yes! I can smell it! I can smell salt!"

"Good boy. Be there soon."

They drove through Dersingham and Snettisham, passing church traffic but little else. Opposite the lavender fields they turned left and wended through the old village of Heacham down to the railway line. Here they parked the car and got out.

"We want to find our bungalow," Lily said.

"Find it? Where is it?"

"It got swept away in the floods. You know, in the spring? It's not our bungalow really, but old Mr Cook who owns it, he always lets us use it for a week after harvest. Only it got swept away."

"Swept away? In the floods?"

"They reckon it got took all the way over the marshes and stopped somewhere up by the station."

Now, as they walked down the road and past the station, they could see gates that were still dragged off their hinges, gardens still brown and overgrown and houses stained half way up their frontage. Odd pieces of wood and metal lay strewn across the marshes and up to the railway line. As they walked parallel to the line a train passed on its way to Hunstanton, whistling and chugging, passengers on their way to their holidays, leaning out of the windows. They walked a hundred yards further and found several heaps of stained white wood, the remains of two or three bungalows, forlorn and abandoned. Bill and Lily thought they recognised one of the heaps; but it might have been another.

"They say they're going to build a sea wall."

"Bit late mebbe."

"Bit late for our bungalow."

They walked slowly back to the car.

"Reckon we need cheering up," Bill said. "Fancy an ice cream, Nicholas?"

"Yeah!"

"Let's get down to the beach and see what there is."

They spent half an hour on the beach but it was too cold to stay longer. Instead, after an ice cream they went to Castle Rising. Nicholas had brought his wooden sword, a Christmas present, and he spent two hours charging up and down the huge mounds of the moat. They ate their picnic: hard boiled eggs, jam sandwiches, half-ripe apples out of the garden and a bit of pork pie. Nicholas thought it was probably one of the best days of his life so far.

Bill brought him home just before tea time. He could hardly walk for fatigue and Bill left him at the door.

"Thank you, Bill!"

"My pleasure. And Lily's. You were a good boy."

Helena heard them and came to the door but Bill had gone.

"Mum! I saw a bungalow that got swept away!"

"Did you?"

"And a big castle! We had a picnic there. It's got dragons!"

"Has it? I never knew that."

"I chased them away."

"How were Bill and Lily? Were they all right?"

"Yeah. They were fine."

"Good. Now, tell me all about it."

"Why, Mum? What's wrong with Bill and Lily?"

"Nothing. I'll tell you afterwards. First, you tell me about your day. Everything, absolutely everything you've done from the moment you left the house."

By the end, he could feel himself drooping. He was too tired for a meal so he had some cornflakes and Helena told him he should go to bed.

"Mum," he said as he stood up.

"Yes, dear?"

32

"Why did you ask about Bill and Lily? You said you'd tell me after."

She paused. "Well, I heard they had a sadness last night."

"What kind of sadness?"

"You didn't know, but they had a child, a boy. He was a little bit younger than you. He was never quite right, you see, even when he was a baby, and he had to stay in a special hospital."

"All the time?"

"Yes, all the time. They visited him every weekend. He probably didn't know who they were, but they always went. This week they went on Saturday. He was very poorly. Then, after they left, I'm afraid he died."

"He died?"

"I'm afraid so, yes. So they must have been very sad."

"Were they sad when they took me out today?"

"Well, they probably were, but going out with you was probably the best thing, you see. It cheered them up."

"Oh. That's good."

FOUR

They worked together silently, the light growing dimmer, the sun sliding away. Nicholas took one row, Helena the next. He had his own, half-sized spade. She had a fork. They worked steadily, not pushing too hard, trying to do just what they could.

In April they had planted the potatoes together. She had made the holes with the dibber, he came behind, dropping in the potatoes, making sure they were the right way up. It had been cold then, bleak and wintry, and it was hard to imagine a whole new plant growing from the one elderly potato. It was tough work to pile up the earth over the potatoes, giving them shelter from the elements. Nicholas remembered that he had been in a crabby mood, unfriendly and defensive. He felt guilty now about it.

As they worked, potatoes arose almost unbidden. They were so plentiful and large that it was hard not to stand on them. It was even harder not to slice them with the spade when digging down into the earth. For some time they had been eating new potatoes, soft and pliable and welcoming. Now they had to dig them all up before the autumn - and before the worm got them. They would leave them on the earth for a day to dry, then bag them up in sacks, wheeling them in the barrow to store in the shed. They hung the sacks from hooks as a precaution against mice.

When she first came to the house, Helena said she knew less about growing vegetables than she did about tiddlywinks in China. Nevertheless she had to learn. The vegetable garden stood waiting at the back, it needed to be filled and if it was not tended it would proliferate with weeds. It was hungry for care and spiteful if neglected. That was what she told her sister Frances, anyway. It was not the language the men on the farm used when she asked their advice. They told her to grow potatoes and onions and low beans and carrots. All of these were easy and none of them needed protection from the birds. Grow marigolds, though, to keep the blackfly away, especially if you grew broad beans. The men offered to come and do it for her but she thanked them and declined. The secret lies in the digging, they told her. Do plenty of digging. Then they explained about rotation of crops.

Through the winter, when it was too cold for any sensible person to be outside, she saw the men going off to work and was shamed into going digging herself. Half an hour per day, she told herself, and she stuck to it. Every now and again she would see Bill or Ernie or John-boy watching her over the hedge. If she was doing it right they said nothing. If she was doing it wrong they still said nothing, but a few days later they might mention, in passing, something about leaving a pathway to stand on, or digging a bit deeper, or raking afterwards.

She and Nicholas were both tired now, their bodies sagging. Without a word she straightened, stretched and looked questioningly at him. She made drinking motions. He grinned. They had done enough for the night. They cleaned their tools and went back to the house.

The day before he went away to school, Nicholas roamed round the farm with Terry. It was hard to believe that in two days he would wake up somewhere different. He had stayed away with Auntie Frances and Uncle Henry and he had stayed at both sets of grandparents but apart from that he had always slept in his own bedroom. Before he left home he wanted to see everything and impress it on his mind lest he should forget.

Terry had already been to school that day. That was another thing: normal school had already gone back. After school, Terry ran all the way to the farm. Harvest had nearly ended; they had finished the barley and were now clearing up the wheat.

There would still be straw to cart but Nicholas would not be doing it. On Saturday Terry might help out.

As they came out of the cattle shed a car drew up in the farmyard. A big, wide, black car.

"Hide! It's Colonel Spencer!"

"Too late!"

Colonel Spencer was a tall, thin man with a long nose and several children. He owned everything as far as the eye could see: he owned the estate. Two of his children were boys and a few were girls, but none of them had ever been to the village school. Colonel Spencer tried to spend as little time as possible with his children and had been heard to say that he hoped the boys would hold a straight bat and a decent gun when they grew older. He held no opinions on the girls. When he opened the car door to get out they were astonished to find that he had one of his daughters beside him.

"Hello, boys," he told them.

"Hello, Colonel Spencer."

"I'm looking for Mrs Hutton."

"She's inside."

"I'll go in."

Colonel Spencer treated all the houses on the estate as if he owned them. Which, of course, he did.

He went up to the back door. His daughter, a plain, red-haired girl, twirled her head in defiance against something and followed him. She ignored the boys. They went in the door.

"Helena!" he called.

"Who's that?"

"Come here a minute!"

Helena emerged into the kitchen brushing her hands. "Why, Andrew! What brings you here? Has war broken out again?" She knew she was safe with sarcasm.

37

"Got a bit of a problem at home. Gussie's gone into hospital. Whip out her appendix so they say. Nanny's on holiday. Cook's day off. The maids only come in the morning. The boys can look after themselves, pick some apples or something to eat. I've put the other girls, what's-their-names, with old Mrs Bulpit for the evening. They can sleep there if needs be, make up an armchair. This one, though, er, Millie, she's a bit old for that. Must be about eleven I should think. Stay here with you for the evening?"

"Well, yes, of course, Andrew. Hello, Millie. I'm a bit busy tonight packing Nicholas' things because he goes away to school tomorrow. But if she doesn't mind that, of course she can stay. The boys can look after her."

"One of those boys is yours?"

"Yes. That's Nicholas there. The other one is Terry, his friend."

"Right-o. I'll be off then. Pick her up later."

"Don't forget." He was gone.

They all stood and stared at each other. Millie did not appear self-conscious or apologetic about falling into their midst. On the other hand she did not seem able to speak.

"Your name Millie?" Terry asked.

She nodded vigorously.

"You live in the hall?"

She nodded again.

"And Colonel Spencer's your dad?"

"Yes." She spoke.

"Where do you go to school?"

38

"I don't go to school." She had a voice unlike anything the boys were used to, clear and fluting as if it might shatter something. They looked at each other.

"Don't go to school? What, never?"

"I have a governess."

They looked at Helena for an explanation.

"That's someone who teaches her at home," she said. "Millie stays at home with her brothers and sisters and they have a classroom there."

"It's called the schoolroom," Millie volunteered.

"You learn sums? And writing?"

"We do literature and music and French. My governess is French so I can speak it quite well."

"Well, tha's a rum'n. There's me going to normal school. There's Nick here going away to school. Then there's her getting the school coming to her. The hell if I know." Terry sat down. It was too much for him.

"Look, boys," Helena said to distract them all. "Why don't you take Millie round the farm? Millie, I don't suppose you've got any gumboots with you or a jersey, have you? Never mind, we'll find you something. Then later we'll get you something to eat but first I've got to finish Nicholas's packing. There's a whole trunk to fill up with clothes. Come with me and we'll find you some boots."

They went out into the sheds. The cattle were out in the fields and the farm was quiet apart from the sound of cats scurrying behind walls, fleeing from human beings or hunting rats and mice. Before they all reached the other side of the farmyard Millie, unaccustomed to her new boots, had fallen over in the mud. It seemed to have no adverse effect. Within minutes she was climbing up heaps of full sacks, rolling down piles of loose corn and mounting ladders into the lofts.

They sat at the top, panting.

"Does your father work for my father?" Millie asked Terry.

"My dad got killed in the war."

"Oh. I see. What about your father, Nicholas? What does he do?"

"He got killed in the war too."

"Oh. My father was in the war."

"Only he wasn't killed."

"No. He was wounded though. At a place called Anzio in Italy. I was very young and I don't remember it."

"I'm going to be a soldier when I grow up."

"So am I," Nicholas said, although he knew it wasn't true.

"What are you going to do?" Terry asked.

"Oh, I expect I shall get married," Millie said. "Then I won't do anything."

The boys looked at each other.

"She could marry you," Terry told Nicholas. This caused great hilarity. They both rolled on the floorboards laughing.

"Or you." They rolled about again. "Or both of us, one at a time."

"I don't see what's so funny," Millie told them. "Everybody gets married."

"Not to him!" Terry yelled, pointing at Nicholas.

"Or him!"

"Just think, getting into bed with her."

"Err, yuck."

"Not like sharing with your brother."

"A girl."

"Be wanting their dolls and that."

"Take up all the room. Kick you out."

"By the way," Millie told them, "I do not have any dolls. I take my book to bed. I'm too old for dolls."

Then Helena called them for supper. Terry went home to get his tea and the others sat down to pigeon pie and apple crumble. Millie was silent again for much of the meal but had two helpings of both courses and declared it to have been the best meal of her life.

Later, Helena told Nicholas that they didn't get much hot food at the hall. Cook was apparently quite capable, but no-one was ever there when the meal was served; they came in when they remembered and scrounged what they could.

Millie went home later and it was eight years before Nicholas saw her again.

FIVE

"Well, hello my dears! You've arrived!"

Helena drove to the new school in their old, black Ford. It took over an hour and was a bit hazardous; she said that next time they might get the train from Swaffham to Bury St Edmunds. Helena had been to visit the school already but to Nicholas it was a complete unknown. They turned in at the gate and rolled up a long, bumpy drive bordered by two huge Wellingtonia trees and a couple of cedars. They parked in front of the main building, a mansion with turrets, gables and French windows, the largest house Nicholas had ever seen.

"Hello, Miles," Helena said. "Hello, Hubert. How nice to see you again. Nicholas, these are Miles and his brother Hubert, your headmasters. You are to call them Miles and Hubert."

"My dear boy," Miles addressed him with a twinkle. "How very nice to see you. We will try to make you completely at home here. Hubert will show you to your dormitory and then we will leave you to matron. Helena, my dear, I hope you will stop for a glass of sherry afterwards."

"Of course."

Nicholas thought that he liked Miles. He seemed funny. He was not so sure about Hubert, a large man with a booming voice who seemed to know Helena from somewhere.

"My dear," Hubert said to Helena, "you look simply angelic. In Norfolk, dusty old Norfolk, you have blossomed. It must be something in the silage. You look not a day older than on your first day at the Footlights with all those randy chaps in charge. What was it Michael Redgrave said about you...?"

"Yes, Hubert, thank you very much. It's fortunate I was always safe with you. Now, what was that you were saying about a dormitory?"

They moved through the double front door into a large hall almost covered in a red and green patterned carpet. Doors led off in all directions, but Hubert led them to the wide main staircase. Nicholas' trunk had been sent by train, to arrive next day, and Helena carried a small suitcase for him with a change of clothes, washing things and a couple of his favourite books.

"You won't walk up this staircase on your own, boy," Hubert told him. "This is for staff. And prefects on a Sunday. You will use the back stairs. But you can come up today. Your dormitory is at the top. It's called the Blue Dormitory. There are also red and green and yellow and senior dorms A and B and then there are the dorms over in the stables."

Nicholas was trying to concentrate but there was a lot to follow. In addition he was transfixed by Hubert's very wide trousers moving ahead of him up the stairs. Inside the trousers must be a very wide bottom. He didn't know any men with such wide bottoms. But they were in Suffolk now, not Norfolk, so maybe that was the reason.

"This is the Blue Dormitory."

Hubert threw open the door. Inside were seven beds. On one of them, in the corner by the window, a small boy sat, crying softly to himself. He looked up with a combination of misery and pleasure, happy that someone had invaded the abyss that he found himself in.

"Ah, this is Willie," Hubert told them by way of explanation. "He's a new boy too. His parents have just gone so you may have to look after him. Matron will soon sort him out. Won't she, Willie?"

Willie made a movement which might have been a nod of assent.

"Well, I'll just let you settle in while I go and greet the other problems," Hubert told them. "And I'll send matron. I'll see you soon, my dears."

Helena placed the suitcase on the bed next to Willie's, which was to be Nicholas', and went to the unhappy boy. She placed an arm round his shoulders and squeezed. It seemed that this brought more tears straight out of him.

"Mum and Daddy went home," Willie sobbed.

"There, there, Willie," she said. "You and Nicholas will have to look after each other, won't you? I'm sure you will be very happy here at school. You'll be playing football and reading nice books and having lovely food and making lots of friends. Your Mummy and Daddy will soon be taking you out as well. Where do you live?"

"I don't like football," Willie said.

"Oh, I'm sure you do really. All boys like football. Do you like cricket? Nicholas loves cricket."

"I don't understand cricket. I like baseball."

"Baseball!" Helena realised that the boy had a twinge of a north American accent. "Are you American?" she asked.

"Not really. We live there now. But I have to go to school here."

"Are your Mummy and Daddy staying here now?"

"No. They're going back tonight. To Cut Bank."

"Cut Bank? Is that near Washington? Is your Daddy a diplomat?"

"It's in Montana. He's a cowboy."

"Oh. A cowboy."

"Yes."

"Well. That's very interesting. Is he in films? Is he an actor?"

"He's a cowboy. He works with cattle. He rides a horse."

"Good Lord. Is he American?"

"Yes. He was in the army. He met Mum in the war. We lived here but then we went to Cut Bank, Montana."

"Where on earth is Montana?"

"I don't know. We just live there."

Helena was stricken suddenly with guilt. She could not imagine that anyone could dump their son half way round the world for an English education - and an expensive one which she imagined was beyond the reach of the average cowboy, from what she knew of cowboys. How could they desert their boy like this?

On the other hand, how could she?

45

She gave Willie another hug. "You and Nicholas will have to be special friends, Willie," she told him. "You will have to come to our house when I take Nicholas out." Then she saw the look of horror that crossed Nicholas' face. "The second time probably, not the first."

"Does he shoot Indians?" Nicholas asked Willie.

"I don't think so. The Indians live on the reservations. They get drunk."

"Does he drive a tractor?"

"He rides a horse."

"Gosh. Mum, Willie's daddy rides a horse."

"Yes, Nicholas."

"I can drive a tractor," Nicholas said.

"You do?"

"Not very well, I must admit. I'm not really big enough. But they need me at harvest for straw carting."

"Right."

"And in the winter I think I'm going to drive it when Bill feeds the cattle with sugar beet tops."

For a moment Nicholas forgot where he was and found himself back at home. Then the door opened and another stranger came in: a big woman with red hair in a white overall.

"Hello," she said. "I'm Matron."

Nicholas and Willie shrank back. Neither of them had ever met anyone like this before.

"Hello Matron," Helena said. "This is Nicholas. Nicholas Hutton. I'm his mother. This is Willie. He was here when we came in. I think he's a bit upset."

"Soon clear that up, Mrs Hutton. No-one here is upset for long. Syrup of figs, that should sort him out. And cod liver oil. We're all very happy here. Now you'll be going along, no doubt. Five other boys coming in here, don't want them all upset. Perhaps Nicholas could see you out, then Nicholas you come back here and we'll unpack your things. Got your football kit? That's all right then. Oh, you'll need to find the back stairs, Hubert never tells you that bit. Fourth on the right."

"Oh. Yes, all right. Well, we'll go to the front door, shall we, Nicholas? Then Matron will help you settle in." She found herself speaking in a voice that Nicholas could hardly recognise, a cross between a military snap and a teenage whine. "Willie, I'll hope to see you again soon. I know you'll be very happy here. You and Nicholas together."

They left. After some searching and even a nervous giggle they found the back stairs. Helena made sure Nicholas could find his way to return and they made their way to the front door. Then she came back with him to the stairs just in case. She kneeled down and gave him a hug that squeezed the air out of him. She felt his arms round her neck and kissed him. "I'll be just across the way for a couple of hours," she said. Miles and Hubert have invited me over for a glass of sherry in that house over there. I won't be far away. Then I'll be thinking about you every minute of every day. And I'll see you very

47

soon for our first outing. I'll bring you home, that's what we'll do. Bye, darling."

Other boys were dashing up and down the stairs now, bigger boys who knew where they were going and what they were doing. Helena could not leave him there. She took him back to the dormitory, opened the door, saw that Matron was still there, smiled at him, kissed him again and left.

Nicholas was shown what to do and eventually went to bed with six other boys in the room. All he could think of was his mother, in the house across the wide path, not yet gone, drinking sherry with Miles and Hubert.

Six

The next morning they had Latin.

Nicholas had a routine in the morning. He touched his teddy bear, then he touched his clock and tried to tell the time. Then he got up and opened the curtains before getting back into bed. If he was still in bed at 7.30 his mother would have come to rouse him but it never happened. He went downstairs to get a drink. Helena then came down in her dressing gown and cooked his breakfast. Afterwards he went upstairs again to change and gather his school things. Helena threw some clothes on and walked him some of the way to school. When he was five she had walked him all the way. Now he did most of it alone.

It was the same every day.

He woke in the dormitory and cried. Neither his teddy bear nor his clock was there. He did not know what the time was. He realised that most of the other boys were crying too. He hoped someone would come and tell them all to do something.

As it happened Matron soon came in and took them to wash, then told them to get dressed. When she took them downstairs to have breakfast he started to feel better.

After breakfast, which they ate in their slippers, they were all directed to the boot room to put on their outdoor shoes. Prefects stood on each corner to shepherd the new boys to all their necessary rendezvous. From the boot room they went outside through the side door, never the front door. In the winter terms they wore their mackintoshes and caps. From the side door they walked round the whole circumference of the grounds, past cedar trees, ponds, lawns and the playing field. It took twenty five minutes. With two minutes to put on their outdoor shoes, two minutes to change back into indoor shoes (not slippers this time) and one minute for unexpected hiccups, it was half an hour between breakfast and assembly.

They went back to the dining room, to their previous places, and were addressed by Miles.

"Now pussycats," he began. "You have all survived those dreadful holidays and have come back bigger, fatter and more stupid. We cannot make you smaller again but we will do our best to make you thinner and cleverer. Eat your greens, kick the ball into the goal and remember your transitive verbs. That will be all. Form One, that is all you new pussycats down there, your first lesson will be Latin with Brigadier Campbell-Wilson. It is in the room next door to here. We call it the dungeon. Try not to be afraid of the brigadier."

Nicholas, Willie and the other new boys shuffled into the next door room, which was dark and a little damp. They stood in the centre of the room wondering whether they were allowed to sit down. From a distance, loud footsteps, born of a heavy tread and crepe soles, steadily approached the door, which was flung open with panache.

"Boys!"

A rumble of responses rose from the dozen small boys.

"Sit down, boys! Find yourselves a desk each!"

They did. The room held twenty desks. Everyone tried to find one at the back.

The brigadier strode to the blackboard. He was dressed in cavalry twill trousers, a tweed jacket, a white shirt and a green tie. He sported a bristling moustache.

"Boys!"

A mumbled response trickled again across the room.

"Boys! When I say "Boys" you reply "Sir"!"

"Sir!"

"You will address me as Sir!"

"Sir!"

"It is not necessary, however, to salute!"

No answer.

"For that you may say "Thank you, sir"!"

"Thank you, sir!"

"And in these lessons you will give me no nonsense!"

"Thank you, sir!"

"I spent twenty years shooting Germans!"

"Thank you, sir!"

"Four years the first time. Not enough. Had to have another go. Took six years the next time."

"Thank you, sir!"

"So I'm not having any nonsense from small boys. Any nonsense, I shoot you!"

"Thank you, sir!"

"Good. So now we understand each other. And for God's sake stop saying "thank you, sir" all the time.

A few mumbles.

"Now boys, we're here to learn Latin."

"Yes, sir!" came from Willie, who seemed to respond to the firm approach.

"I am going to write the following words on the board and I want you to copy them down on the exercise books which I hope you all have."

Fortunately they had. The brigadier turned to the board and wrote in chalk:

Verb

Noun

Preposition

Conjunction

Subject Nominative

Object Accusative

Genitive Dative Ablative

Transitive

Intransitive

Phrase

Clause

Singular

Plural

Tense

"Can you all read and write? Anyone who can't do both, fall out here!"

No-one fell out. However, behind Nicholas came a muffled sound of weeping from a small boy called Whiskin Minor. Nicholas already knew that the reason he was called Minor was because he had an older brother in the school.

"Yes, boy?"

Whiskin Minor had raised his hand. However, no further sound arose from him so the brigadier stamped round the classroom to his side.

"Ah," he said. "An irrigation problem I see."

Whiskin Minor whimpered. All the other boys shrank into their desks. Would he shoot Whiskin Minor?

"Ah," said the brigadier again. "Ah. Well, never mind, boy. Worse things happened at Dunkirk, let me tell you." He reflected a minute. "Far worse, actually.

"Still, only natural. Faced with the enemy, barrage balloons up, shells flying over, trench mortars, what have you, natural reaction from a chap. Saw it all the time in the trenches. And the Blitz. All you need is a change of kit, boy, be good as new."

"Yes, sir. Thank you, sir."

"Now you just report to the quartermaster, boy. To the matron, that is. You know where the matron is stationed?"

"Y-yes, sir. I think so, sir."

"Mmm. Fact is, I think I'll take you there myself in case you lose your bearings. The rest of you boys, you copy out all those words from the board, you understand?"

"Yes, sir!"

"And someone copy out an extra list for this boy while we're gone. What's your name, boy?"

"W-Whiskin Minor, sir."

"Whiskin Minor, eh? And do you have a first name?"

"Andrew, sir."

"Well, Andrew Whiskin Minor, do you have any idea what a transitive verb is?"

"N-no, sir."

"Right then, Andrew Whiskin Minor, you come with me and we'll soon get you shipshape and fit for parade, won't we, boy? And before you know where you are, transitive verbs will be like your second cousins, do you understand?"

"I-I think so, sir."

"Good for you, boy. Now let's go and find matron."

The brigadier flung open the door, turned round and glowered at the class and made his exit with Whiskin Minor. The rest of the boys copied down his words, none of which they had ever heard of before.

In the main hall was a timetable, incomprehensible at first but colour coded so that each class knew where they were supposed to be at which time. Some of the boys could not tell the time so the schedule was carefully printed in order of lessons; if you could remember what you just had, you knew where to go next. There was an order to the lessons which Nicholas found helpful. He liked being told what to do.

On the first afternoon they were told to change into their football clothes. First they went to the clothes cupboard, where matron gave them their green football socks, blue shirts and white shorts. They were given a yellow shirt as well to take with them, as they could not all play on the same side. The shorts were woolly and rubbed against the skin; the boys would later discover that on wet days they chafed and chapped their legs. They were all told to put the sports clothes in their own games lockers after football. They would be washed on Mondays.

There were two football pitches, North Pitch and South Pitch. The big boys played on North Pitch and Nicholas and his class were directed to South Pitch, where Mr Blacksmith awaited them.

Mr Blacksmith was a tall, dark, spindly young man who looked as if he had insufficient strength to kick a football himself. He taught geography and scripture to the older boys; Nicholas' class was thought too young for either subject. He smiled gently at the twenty five boys surrounding him.

"Well, boys," he said as loudly as he could. "We're all here to play football, aren't we?"

"Yes, sir!"

"Jolly good. I think we'd better pick up sides then. Can any of you count?"

"Yes, sir!"

"Jolly good. How many boys are there here?"

Furious counting went on until an approximate number was agreed on.

"Well done, boys. First task accomplished. Who wants to play in goal? We can't have two goalies on the same side."

No-one came forward.

"Jolly good, boys. We'll take it in turns, then. Now I think I'll pick the sides. When I say Stanley Matthews you go over here. When I say Tom Finney you go over there. Understood, boys?"

They didn't really but eventually they separated into nearly equal numbers.

"Tiger!" A cry came from across the field.

"Yes, Miles?" To Nicholas' surprise, the answer came from Mr Blacksmith. He was apparently Tiger.

"Get the pussycats running about or they'll catch the palsy."

"Just starting, Miles. They're straining at the leash." He turned to them all. "Now, boys, when I blow the whistle you've got to run about like anything, otherwise you'll get the palsy and I'll get into trouble with Miles. O.K.? You and you, you're in goal to start with. We'll change you every five minutes. Now, Stanley Matthews down that end, Tom Finney up this end. Go!"

They all ran down to their respective ends. Mr Blacksmith did not bother giving them positions but selected a boy to kick off. Then all twenty five boys chased after the ball in a pack.

Nicholas loved football. He loved it almost as much as cricket. He wasn't sure he was very good at it but there was always time to improve. Mr Goodbody had told him that Willie Watson, who played cricket for England that year, had also played football for England. That was Nicholas' main aim.

He ran after the ball with the others. At first he could not get near it for the horde, but after a few minutes he found that the numbers thinned. Some of the boys had fallen over and never got up again. Others simply sat down. The ball went backwards and forwards, never approaching either of the goals, and a few boys still chased it. Above all, Mr Blacksmith still chased it. It turned out that he could run like the wind.

Then he blew the whistle and called all the boys around him.

"Well, boys," he said. "That was a very good start. However, I think some of you boys have been eating lots of dumplings over the summer holidays. And you were so busy eating dumplings that you didn't have any time for running about. But some of you have been running about and not eating dumplings, and that's very good. Now I think we'll put you all in positions so you don't have to run about so much. Oh dear, what have we here?"

Willie, Nicholas' dormitory neighbour, had moved to the touch-line and was lying on the grass, face down, shaking with sobs.

"Hello, young man," Mr Blacksmith said to him genially. "Don't you like football much?"

"I'm frightened," Willie told him with honesty.

"There, there. It's only a beastly old football, old man. It doesn't go very fast and it's not poisonous. Still, if you're a bit frightened that's important. Do you play football at home?"

"I play baseball at home."

"Do you now? That's very eccentric. You must teach me how to play. I don't think I know your name, by the way. I'm called Mr Blacksmith. What are you called?"

"Willie."

"Willie? That's a nice name. Do you know what your second name is?"

"Peter."

"Ah yes. What I meant to say was, do you have a, well, third name? A surname? Never mind, Willie is good enough. I tell you what, how about if you help me with the refereeing? Would you like to blow the whistle for me to save my puff? When I say blow, you blow like anything. How would that be?"

For a few moments a very dubious silence emanated from Willie. Then Mr Blacksmith gave him the whistle. He blew on it, tentatively at first, then louder.

"Louder!" cried Mr Blacksmith.

Willie blew it louder.

"Louder!"

Willie blew it till everyone looked round from the other game.

"That's enough!" Mr Blacksmith told him. "Right, chaps, let's get on with it now you've all got your puff back. What's the score? Oh yes, there isn't one. Let's see what we can do about that."

SEVEN

Nicholas' first outing fell on a Sunday at the end of September. The boys went to church wearing their mackintoshes and caps. When they returned, a number of cars stood near the main door to the school, waiting to carry away those who had outings. Nicholas saw the old black Ford at the corner of the drive.

He ran across the drive at flat out speed and threw himself at his mother. She grasped him round the waist, pulled him to her and kissed the top of his head, time after time.

"Nicholas, you're bigger! It's only been three weeks and you're bigger!"

"Mum, can we go home?"

"Of course we can, dear. Of course we can. Just as soon as I can let go of you. You look so good I want to eat you up. Oh, it's been so quiet without you."

"Mum, Miles says I'm going to be the new Oscar Wilde. Who was Oscar Wilde?"

Helena burst out laughing. "I hope he means for the quality of your English. Oscar Wilde was a playwright, dear. A very clever man. You must be doing well."

"And Mr Blacksmith says I'm like Tom Finney on the football field. Who's Tom Finney?"

"I don't know so much about Tom Finney, darling, although I know he plays for England. And I know Stanley Matthews won the Cup Final for Blackpool this year."

"And I want to climb Mt Everest when I grow up, like Edmund Hillary and Sherpa Tensing!"

"Perhaps you will, dear. You've obviously been very busy, anyway. Let's get in the car and you can tell me all about it on the way home."

It was an hour's drive and they never stopped talking for one moment; or at least Nicholas never stopped talking. Before they knew it they had arrived.

"What's for lunch?"

"Toad in the hole, is that all right?"

"Smashing! Is Bill there today?"

"It's Sunday, isn't it? He fed the cattle this morning. I expect someone will be over to do the milking later."

"I hope it's Bill.

Helena stopped the car outside the house. For a moment complete stillness fell; then Nicholas tore out of the car and ran straight upstairs to his bedroom. Everything seemed to be in the right place: his teddy bear, his cricket bat, his tractor and his books. He ran down again and saw that almost everything downstairs was unchanged. A new waste paper basket stood in the sitting room and a new cup and saucer stood on the draining board. He ran outside and round the farm sheds. All seemed the same. Sugar beet tops filled the two wheeled trailer; the sugar beet harvest had started since he went away.

"You're like a cat," Helena laughed. "You want to establish your territorial rights. Don't start weeing everywhere, will you?"

"What's for lunch?"

"I already told you. Toad in the hole."

"Oh yes. What are we going to do this afternoon?"

"Well, we can go for a walk if you like, just to see that everything's still the same. Or we can play cards or draughts or Monopoly. Or you can play with your toys. Whatever you like, you're in charge today."

"I think we'll do all of them!"

"That's fine. Then we'll have a bit of tea and we must get you back for six o'clock before your meal at school."

"Six o'clock! What time do we have to leave here then?"

"About five."

"Oh no - we've only just got here! I shall have to do everything very fast."

"You will, dear. We'll get everything done though. Now let me get the lunch. It won't take long, I've prepared it already. Go and play with your toys for a few minutes."

Toad in the hole was followed by fruit salad from a tin and condensed milk. Helena had a cup of coffee and Nicholas a glass of pop. Then they went out for a walk behind the field.

"Mum?"

"Yes, dear?"

"Miles says you were quite well known before the war. Is that true?"

She laughed. "Yes, Nicholas, I suppose that's fairly true. I was moderately well known. I wasn't really famous though. Then I met your father and I became a country lady and had you instead, which was much better."

"Miles says Denis Compton is the greatest sportsman in the country. Mr Goodbody only said he was the greatest cricketer."

"They may both be right, darling. I wouldn't know."

"And Miles says there's an iron curtain in Europe. What's an iron curtain, Mum?"

"It means it's like an iron curtain. The Russians have taken over all the countries in the east of Europe like Poland and Hungary and they won't let anyone out."

"Gosh. You know Willie Dodger?"

She hesitated for one moment. "That's Willie who sleeps next to you?"

"Yes, well, his dad really is a cowboy. Only he's got his own ranch. His mum she got some money because her parents got killed in the war by a bomb and they were quite rich, they lived in Kent but the Germans dropped some bombs there on the way home from bombing London and they hit their home and they were killed."

"That's terrible."

"But then Willie's mum, she already met this cowboy, Mr Dodger, when he was in the army here, so she had to go back to

America with him but she wanted Willie to get a proper education so he's come over here. He says tomayto and gosh darn it and he said a very funny word the other day, it was vee-hickle, and Brigadier Campbell-Wilson made him spell it on the blackboard because he said he'd got no idea what he was talking about. Only Willie couldn't spell it properly anyway but Brigadier Campbell-Wilson said he'd got the gist now and then he laughed. Matron says when the Brig laughs she thinks there's been an earthquake somewhere in the grounds."

"The Brig? Are you allowed to call him that?"

"We have to call him sir when he's there. We call him the Brig when he's not there. He was in two wars, Mum. He stayed in the army all the time after the first one. He's been all over the world. He was in India. And Dunkirk. And Alamein."

"His poor wife, did she go with him all the time or was she left at home?"

"She wasn't at Dunkirk, Mum, don't be silly. She went to India though. He calls her the memsahib. He spelled it on the board for us. Only the officers got their wives in India, the men had to leave them at home."

"I bet they did. Accounts for all the Anglo-Indians springing up everywhere. Right, do we turn back now? Bill might be there soon."

When they approached the farm Nicholas began running. As he turned the corner into the yard he saw Bill's bicycle leaning against a post. He tore into the cow sheds and saw Bill, getting the feed ready before he fetched the cows.

Nicholas stood stock still. For a moment Bill could not see him against the light.

"Nicholas? Young Nick?"

Nicholas was unable to move for sheer happiness. He felt himself laughing but was unable to control it.

Bill came over to him. "Lost your tongue eh, Nick? The cat got it? Tha's a rum job, you go away to school to get educated and you come back and can't talk." He came across further, put his arm round Nicholas' shoulder and gave him the hardest squeeze he had ever had in his life. "Well, you'd better help me get the cows in, then. Don't have to talk for that. I'm now going."

"BILL!"

"Oh, you can still talk, then?"

"BILL!"

"Can't say anything but Bill, though. Funny old school that, don't hardly teach you anything except how to say Bill. Waste of money I'd say. Learn more in this shed."

"Can we get the cows in?"

"I just said how we'd get the cows in. Come you on, master. I've finished the feed. Cows are on the Old Meadow. Let's see what they've got to say for themselves. Probably got a few words to say about you coming home, I'd reckon."

"Do you understand what they say, Bill?"

"Me? Course I do. Every word."

"What do they say?"

"Oh, they talk about the weather, you know, and the grass, and if it's time for milking. And football of course. Gertie, that old Aberdeen Angus, she loves her football. We read the paper together in the morning, she wants to know all the scores. Specially the Scottish ones, her being from Aberdeen."

They walked off to the Old Meadow.

EIGHT

Dear Mum,

I nerly scored a goal in football yesterday. It went past the post. I got nine out of ten for spelling with Miss Fortune. Her name isn't really Miss Fortune it's Miss Smith but Miles calls her Miss Fortune. Miles says I look like the Sar of Rusher. We had chips for tea last nigt. And fish. Thank you for the outing it was lovly. Can't wait for Christmas. Love from Nicholas.

—

Dear Nicholas,

Thank you very much for your lovely letter. I have got one big piece of news to tell you. Bill has got a dog. It's a collie, which is quite a large sheepdog. He brings it to work with him and takes it in the fields but he asks if I could look after it sometimes when he is working. It cries if he leaves it at home and Lily's out. I shouldn't keep calling her "it". She's a girl dog. Her name is Hettie and she's lovely. Anyway, you will see her soon, perhaps on your next outing.

She's still only a puppy really and very affectionate. I know you'll love her and she'll love you.

I have been asked to do a bit of acting work. Mr Wolfit, whom I have mentioned to you, has asked if I will work for him in Nottingham, Sheffield, Manchester and Newcastle on a tour. I have also been asked to appear in a film but I'm not sure about this yet. Of course I shall only work during the term time and I will be able to take you on all your outings. I have told them that I can't ever work during the school holidays. I shall spend all of them here with you. Then if I am away in the term time I shall write to you from wherever I'm working and you can write back to me there.

We're having a big bonfire in the village on Guy Fawkes Night. I don't think they have ever done this before but fireworks cost a lot of money and some people can't afford to buy their own. I'm not sure what day of the week November 5th is but we'll have to see if you can come.

Auntie Frances is coming here to stay next week for a couple of days. Uncle Henry is staying at home for most of the time because he's working. He has got a new job on the Observer, the Sunday paper. He has to get people to write about new books for the paper, so it's a very good job. He might come up on Sunday with Auntie Frances and stay until Monday. Oh, I nearly forgot to tell you. She's going to have a baby! That will be your cousin! It will be a young cousin for you to look after. If it's a boy you can teach him to play cricket and football when he's old enough. If it's a girl, well, you can take her to places and be like a big brother. Auntie Frances is going to have the baby in about five months' time. That will be just about the same time as Bill's cows start having calves!

Well, what else have I been doing? I went into King's Lynn the other day. You know the big market on a Tuesday? I went all round the stalls to buy some vegetables, which was good fun. Then I parked the car outside Smith's on the High St and bought two books. They're a bit old for you. One is a fairly new one by someone called William Cooper and the other one came out at the start of the war but I've never read it. It's called How Green Was My Valley, by Richard Llewellyn.

I have just had a cup of tea and a cigarette and now I'm going to have lunch. I shall write to you next week and then it will be time for your next outing. It will be lovely to see you then.

All my love,

Mum

NINE

It was a Saturday morning when Miles strode demonstratively into breakfast. Everyone could see that he was in a bate because he was wearing his green corduroy jacket. The light brown one, slightly faded, signalled a good mood. The green one suggested staying out of his way.

Nicholas was not automatically frightened of Miles. Hubert was a different matter; he could explode without warning and had been known to knock a boy across the room with one slap. Miles, on the other hand, was more predictable. He was also generous and funny so that, when he hit you, you felt it was inevitable because of your behaviour and probably you deserved it.

"Silence!" Miles spoke tersely and it was not necessary to raise his voice. The room was nearly silent already.

"Armitage," he said.

"Yes, Miles?" Armitage, twelve years old, a star centre forward in the football team, very clever and very popular, stood up.

"Sit down." He sat.

"Armitage, I have been reading your Scripture composition. I have found three commas. Not one, not two. Three commas."

No answer from Armitage but it looked as if he shook slightly.

"You are forbidden to use commas, are you not?"

"Yes, Miles."

"As you know, commas herald the downfall of the English language. Particularly commas as used wantonly by you."

"Yes, Miles."

"In your Scripture composition for Mr Blacksmith you have inserted three commas into your description of the Sermon On The Mount."

No answer.

"Have you not?"

"I... I don't remember, Miles."

"Mr Blacksmith has influenza and so I have marked the papers. Mr Blacksmith may not have known of the proscription on employing commas but I do."

"Yes, Miles."

"Are you able to explain yourself?"

"I... thought -"

"You're not here to think, boy, you're here to be educated. Do you have a satisfactory explanation?"

"I may have been describing a list of things..."

"Then don't describe lists of things! You will not use commas in my school!"

"No, Miles."

"There is plenty of time to be clever when you grow up. Your task while you are at this school is to learn to conduct yourself like a civilised human being."

"Yes, Miles."

"Come with me."

A shivering Armitage rose from the table, made his way between his neighbours and followed Miles into the staff drawing room next door. He closed the door behind him. A few moments later the boys heard the terrible swish of the cane, three times. One for each comma. After a couple of minutes Armitage re-emerged into the dining room, ashen. One tear trickled down the side of his nose. He sat down again, very, very gently. One of his neighbours poured him a drink but he could neither eat nor drink for the rest of breakfast.

For the third outing of term Nicholas took Willie home with him. He was not keen but Helena persuaded him that it would be kind; Willie appeared to have no family in Britain who were prepared to take him out and he spent his weekends walking round the school grounds or playing board games. Nicholas wanted to go home on his own, to go to his bedroom and see his toys, then explore the farm buildings, find out what was new and perhaps play for a time with Terry. Now he would have to be kind.

Helena was waiting when they came from church. Nicholas ran to her and hugged her. He still had great difficulty in understanding why he could not see her every day. Willie came over and stood near them.

"Hello, Willie. How nice to see you. I'm so glad you can come out with Nicholas today."

"Hello, Mrs Hutton." Willie moved from one foot to the other.

"Now, I think you boys should have a race to see who can get changed fastest. The winner gets a boiled sweet."

They hared off to their dormitory, tore off their grey flannel shorts and white shirts and put on corduroys and green shirts. They ran down again, Nicholas leading by a length. Helena gave him a boiled sweet then gave Willie one too. They climbed quietly into her car, Nicholas sitting in front.

"Ma'am, what kind of motorcar is this?"

"This is a Ford, Willie. Some kind of Ford."

"Does it always make that kind of noise?"

"I'm afraid it does. It rattles a little bit. Like the rattlesnake. I hope it will get us home, though."

"Maybe we won't be able to get back here again!" Nicholas said eagerly.

"I expect we'll manage somehow. Now, Willie, what would you like to do for your day out?"

This flummoxed Willie, who had no idea what he would like to do for his day out.

"I expect you'd like to see the farm, wouldn't you? See if it's like the ranch at home? We haven't got any horses, I'm afraid. The farmers go round on tractors here."

"We have tractors too, ma'am. But we use horses when we round up the cattle."

"Of course you do. By the way, you don't have to call me ma'am, Willie. We don't usually say that in England. It's nice of you, though, and very polite."

"Mum, Willie's a referee now."

"A referee? At football?"

"Yes, he referees all our games. He's better at reffing than playing, you see."

The journey passed in discussion of football, farming and food. Helena had put a joint in the oven before leaving and it was due to be ready when they returned. She still had to boil potatoes and cabbage and make the gravy, so they had enough time to go round the farm before eating.

"Oh, and by the way, Nicholas, I hope you don't mind but I've invited a friend of mine for lunch. He's called Bernard Coombs. He'd like to meet you."

A man as well as Willie. Still, at least they were both on the same day. This might mean that next time there would be no-one.

"Of course I don't mind, Mum. Is he a farmer? Does Bill know him?"

"No, he's a sort of banker. He puts money, his own money, into shows and plays and things. He's come to talk to me about a play. Whether I want to be in it, that sort of thing."

"Oh. All right."

The meeting with the banker, however, was postponed until after farm exploration. As the car came to a halt in the farmyard, with a cry of "Come on!" Nicholas flung open a door and the boys ran to the sheds. They opened one gate after another, always punctiliously closing them afterwards, until they had been through every yard. He explained that the cows would be coming in later and that, even at this time of year, the bullocks would be staying in the fields; only in the depths of winter did they go into the yards. He took Willie round the pig sheds where huge old sows snorted at them and ran up hoping for food; instead the boys scratched their backs. They examined the hay sheds and sacks of food, the cats, the rats and the pigeons which Bill occasionally caught for a pie. Willie said it was smaller than he was used to, and warmer. At this time in Cut Bank they had thick snow, the ice particles froze inside your nose and the steers were all dead. They would be replaced next year. The heifers were kept indoors for breeding and the winter was spent recovering, patching up and waiting for the spring. Sometimes they would go walking with snow shoes in Glacier National Park. Apart from that they only went outside to walk to their vehicles.

Helena called them from the back door and they ran back across the yard. She was waiting inside the back door. They took off their outdoor shoes and she still waited, apparently in suspense. Then she led them to the kitchen.

"Nicholas, this is my friend Mr Coombs. You can call him Bernard if you like."

Mr Coombs was relaxing in a winged chair at the kitchen table. He was a tall, mildly florid man with a slight moustache, dressed in a brown suit, a v-necked pullover, a flannel shirt and a plain tie. As the boys came in he rose, took off his jacket and extended his hand. Nicholas shied away momentarily and then shook it. Mr Coombs was very tall.

"And this is Nicholas' friend, Willie."

"Pleased to meet you, Willie." He shook Willie's hand too.

"Mr Coombs - Bernard - is here to discuss a play with me, as I told you."

"Yes... a play your mother might be in. We've been talking money."

"Now, won't you all sit down and I'll put the lunch on the table. Nicholas, in your usual seat. Willie, over there please. Do you want some pop, boys?"

"Yes, Mum!"

For a while food took precedence over conversation. Helena sprang up and down to fetch things; even when everything was on the table she seemed unable to settle. Bernard Coombs looked around him at her and at the boys. Nicholas and Willie ate keenly. Willie had never previously encountered Yorkshire pudding but came back for more. They had second glasses of pop. Finally replete, they wiped their mouths with napkins and sat back.

"Enough, boys?"

"That was smashing, Mum."

"Thank you very much, Mrs Hutton. That was the best meal I ever had in my life."

"Oh, I don't think so, Willie." She laughed politely. "But thank you anyway. We'll wait a few minutes and have some pudding. We've got fruit salad and condensed milk."

"There's more?" Bernard asked. "My God, I think I'll come back again next week. If invited, of course." Helena laughed nervously. "Mind you, I'd like to be invited."

"Can I ask you something, sir?" Willie requested suddenly.

"Of course."

"How do you spell your name? Coombs?" They realised that Willie was having trouble pronouncing the word. With his mid-England, mid-Montana inflexions it came out somewhere near comes and combs, but nowhere did the double vowel meet the consonants satisfactorily. His question was a real one, born of a desire to be polite.

Bernard spelled it for him.

"Oh... I never knew that."

"It's a funny name, I know. We British have lots of strange names, I'm afraid. What's your second name?"

"Dodger."

A moment's silence hung over the table like a small grenade. Then Bernard exploded in laughter.

"Dodger! Oh, I'm sorry! What an unfortunate name. Mr and Mrs Dodger and all the little Dodgers!" He roared again.

Willie looked across at him, crimson, then averted his face in dismay.

"Now, Bernard," Helena intervened. "It's not that funny. In fact it's not funny at all. I'm sure it's a perfectly normal name where Willie comes from, isn't it, Willie?"

Willie did not respond.

Nicholas was bemused. He knew Willie's name, of course, but he was not aware of anything strange about it. What was so funny?

"Why don't we have the fruit salad later, boys, before you go back? Off you go and play now while I clear up. Bernard, you can dry up if you would."

"He should dry up," Nicholas said to Willie as they went out. "Shall we let his tyres down?"

"Is that his motor car?"

"It must be." They went over to a red Commer saloon standing at the edge of the farmyard. Nicholas looked in the back window and saw a small brown suitcase; he wondered why Mr Coombs had brought a suitcase when he had only come for lunch.

They ran again across the farmyard. Willie was quiet for a while but recovered when they began climbing over the trailers. Later they would help Bill feed and milk the cows.

On the way back to school they were subdued.

"Mum?" Nicholas asked.

"Yes, dear?"

"Will Mr Coombs be coming again?"

"I'm not sure, darling. Why?"

"Nothing."

"Are you sure? Weren't you very keen on him?"

"Well..."

"He was a bit off with Willie, did you mean?"

"A bit."

"Don't worry, Nicholas, I won't let anyone be rude to you or your friends."

"Thanks, Mum."

Nicholas never saw Bernard Coombs again after that.

TEN

On the last day of term, after they had had their tea, Nicholas went to see Miles in his study. For half an hour after tea, Miles was available to all the boys. He had a glass of sherry by his side and he puffed intermittently on a Turkish cigarette. Outside his door hung a revolving sign saying alternatively Yes No Wait, which he said he had borrowed from Denis Compton calling for a single. At the moment it said Yes. Nicholas knocked.

"Enter!"

Miles was facing away from him, writing on a pad on his desk. All the furniture in the room was dark, heavy, oak or mahogany, and most of it was large. Books lined the walls, principally Dickens and Wisden Cricketers' Almanack. The central light was not switched on but Miles had two desk lamps creating a pool of light around his head. His shadow flickered against the walls behind him.

"Come in, pussycat. Sit down." Miles continued with his work without looking round to see who it was.

Nicholas sat at a chair nearly parallel with the desk. Miles signed his name and turned round. "Ah, it's you, pussycat. Looking forward to going home?"

"Yes, Miles."

"Good boy. Not too much sherry and Christmas pudding, remember. Now then, what did you want?"

"Please, Miles... "

"Yes, dear?"

"I don't really want to come back here again."

Miles turned his chair round. "Don't you, dear?"

"Not really, no."

"Is it the food? Is Miss Fortune nasty to you?"

"The food's very nice. Miss Fortune is very, very nice. Everyone's very nice. But I miss my home, Miles." He could feel a prickling behind his eyes. His nose began to run and he pulled out his handkerchief to blow it. "I was going to ask if you would tell Mummy not to send me back here again."

A bit of a pause fell. Then Miles found a spare glass and the bottle of sherry and poured a little into it. "You're getting to be a big pussycat now," he said. "It's time you had a glass of sherry."

"Can I have a cigarette too?"

"No, you can't!" Then he saw that Nicholas was joking. "Nicholas, you're too young to have a sense of humour," he said. "Leave the jokes to your elders and betters, please. What are you reading, child?"

"Er, Gimlet King of the Commandos. And Captain Marryat. And Little Dorrit."

"Little Dorrit, eh? Do you understand it?"

"Some of it. Not much." The school library was full from door to wall of books that the children could take whenever they wanted. Nicholas had been browsing.

"Do you like detective stories?"

"I haven't read any. I read the Scarlet Pimpernel."

"Well done. Now let me lend you two books for the holidays. This one here is by Rex Stout. It's called The Golden Spiders. Then there is this other one by Raymond Chandler, The Big Sleep. Oh, and take this one by Dashiell Hammett, The Thin Man. Tell me what you think of them next term. If you don't like them we'll burn them."

"Gosh. Thank you, Miles."

"Not at all. You may be rather a clever puss, Nicholas. I think you may do quite well. Your mother thinks so too. I believe she's going to be in a play next term. Perhaps we can arrange a trip to see it."

"Gosh. Thank you, Miles."

"Have a good Christmas, pussycat. And tell me what you think of those books. Don't worry if you don't understand them. Nor do I."

Nicholas had taken a small sip of his sherry but he left the rest. It was disgusting.

He woke in his own bed.

He was back in the rhythm of his life. It was a word he had learned only recently but it seemed to suit his surroundings. He woke at seven, when it was still dark. He lay quietly for a while, planning the day, then got out of bed to switch on the light. It was freezing. Condensation steamed the windows and a sliver of ice lined the bottom corner. He grabbed his book and burrowed back under the covers.

At quarter to eight his mother called from outside his room and put her head round the door. "Are you awake? Are you ready for breakfast?"

"Yes!"

"Get washed and dressed then. Clean your teeth. I'll cook your breakfast. Do you want fried bread?"

"Yes!"

"I bet you have to say please at school."

"If we don't we get our hands slapped."

"Maybe I should do the same."

"Mum!" They both laughed.

Helena read the paper at breakfast, nibbled at a piece of fried bread, drank a cup of coffee and smoked a cigarette. Nicholas read his book.

"What's that you're reading, dear?"

"Miles lent it to me. It's called The Big Sleep. I don't know where the sleep comes in yet. It's by someone called Raymond Chandler."

"Chandler! The Big Sleep! Miles lent you that? At eight years old?

"He said I might not understand it all."

"I should hope not. It's very unsuitable." She laughed. "You're supposed to be reading Enid Blyton, aren't you? Or at least Arthur Ransome."

"I hate Enid Blyton. This is much better. It's more like real life."

"Not yours, I hope. Or mine. Well, I suppose there's something to be said for an all round education. Why did Miles lend you it? Had you run out of books?"

Nicholas hesitated. "I told him I didn't want to come back to school again."

Helena put down her paper. "Did you, Nicholas? Why was that? Has someone been unkind to you?"

"No. They've all been very nice. But I miss home, Mummy. I miss you."

"Oh, I'm so sorry, darling." She went round and wrapped him in her arms. "It must be awful for you."

Nicholas, though, found he was in no danger of shedding tears now, at home. "Yes, it is rather," he said matter of factly. "But I suppose that makes it lovely when I come home."

"What did Miles say?"

"He didn't really say anything. He gave me a glass of sherry, which was disgusting, and lent me the books. He said if I didn't like them we'd burn them."

Helena laughed again. "Good old Miles. He hasn't changed much. You know I used to know him before the war. Him and Hubert. I knew Hubert better, I suppose. In the theatre. They both did a bit of acting but Miles was more of a producer really. Hubert used to be in reviews. He was at Cambridge, in the Footlights, and they came to London."

"Were you in reviews too?"

"Yes, about 1935, before I got some good parts in plays. We had a nice time then, it was a lot of fun."

"Was he your boyfriend then?"

"No! Hubert wasn't really interested in girls, Nicholas. Nor was Miles."

"Not at all?"

"No, I don't think so. They've got other things on their mind."

"Like plays and books?"

"Something like that, yes."

They went back to their reading for a while and Helena finished her coffee.

"So do you think you can manage to go back to school again, Nicholas?"

A man had just come through a door with a gun in his hand, but after a moment Nicholas looked up.

"It means you can go back to work, doesn't it, Mum?"

"Well, it may do, dear, but that's not the point. If you're going to be unhappy we won't do it. It's not worth it."

Nicholas had been saving the last piece of cold fried bread. He picked it up and chewed it, savouring the soggy juiciness of it, moving it around in his mouth.

"I think it'll be all right, Mum," he said. "I think Miles is very nice most of the time. Except when he gets in a bate. Then he hits us."

"He hits you? Hard?"

"Quite hard. Round the head. Not like Hubert though. He knocked Willie over once. Miles sort of smacks us. Or sometimes he beats you with a cane. But he hasn't done that to me yet."

"My God." Helena put down her paper and stared at her son. With some difficulty she lit another cigarette. "You're telling me the truth, Nicholas? They really hit you like that?"

"Yes, Mum, course. We don't often see Hubert though. He doesn't teach us. He does office work I think."

"Do the other teachers hit you too?"

"The Brig did once. Not me. He gave Henry Thomas a clip. They're called Brig clips. Henry was eating chewing gum in class. When the Brig gave him a clip his chewing gum went straight out of his mouth on his desk. Everyone laughed, even the Brig. But he doesn't usually hit anyone. Nor does Tiger. Mr Blacksmith, Miles calls him Tiger. He says he wants to keep us quiet by using his thoughts."

They did some more reading.

"Nicholas," Helena said, looking up, "are you absolutely sure you don't mind going back again after Christmas?"

"Fairly sure, Mum. It's probably for the best. I can get a good education and you can do some work to pay for it. And I can always see you in the theatre if they take us to one of your plays."

"But you hate seeing me in plays, don't you? And I don't blame you."

No answer seemed to be necessary to that, so Nicholas stayed silent. He finished his fried bread, drank some tea and carried on with his book. If he could understand it a bit better he thought it might become his favourite book, superseding Gimlet King of the Commandos.

Eleven

They spent Christmas with Auntie Frances and Uncle Henry. They still had no children, a state of affairs which would not last for much longer. On the minus side, there was no-one to play with. On the plus side, there was no competition for the skin off the custard or the cream off the milk or the attention of the adults. Nicholas was the king of the party. He knew he was being spoiled. He tried not to exploit the situation but he did enjoy it. When they came home again it was strange getting used to normal life.

On the following Sunday snow lay on the ground. The cattle would need more feed than usual and Bill or Ernie would be coming round. Within the next few days, and earlier if the snow remained, they would get the cattle in for the winter. On that first Sunday, though, Bill was there with the tractor at eight o'clock.

Nicholas was waiting at the window. He pulled on his boots, a jacket and his gloves and ran outside. Immediately he fell over in the icy farmyard, scraping his knees below his short trousers. He picked himself up again and ran across to the shed.

"Good morning, Nick," Bill told him. "Have a nice trip?"

The joke was lost on Nicholas. "We went to Auntie Frances's house," he said. "Bill, can I come feeding? Can I go on the trailer?"

"Course you can. How am I going to manage if you never? You sure your knees are all right? Not bleeding?"

"They're all right." As a fact his knees were bleeding, but it was nothing unusual. He climbed up on the two-wheeled trailer, where the sugar beet tops were already loaded. Snow covered the top layer in frozen blocks. Bill started the tractor and they went to the field just behind the farm.

It was freezing. Bill would not let Nicholas use a pitchfork, which anyway was too big for him. He had to pick up the tops by hand and throw them over the side. The bullocks came running to the trailer and followed it down the field, chewing on the tops behind it and then running up to the trailer again. After two minutes Nicholas' hands were almost solid with cold and his nose was icy. He continued trying to pick up bunches of sugar beet tops but it was too much for him. His eyes streamed, though whether from cold or tears it was hard to say.

Bill stopped the tractor and climbed down. "Them gloves of yours," he said, "you're about as much use as a girl from London with them. Here, come on down."

He helped Nicholas jump from the trailer. "You remember how to drive the tractor? Same as straw carting. I put it in gear, you just cop on the wheel and steer her. Don't even need to put your foot on the clutch until I say so. Keep her steady."

As the tractor moved slowly across the field with Nicholas steering in first gear and with low throttle, Bill climbed on the drawbar and over the front of the trailer. Using a four-tine fork he tipped the rest of the tops over for the cattle. He called out instructions to steer towards the gate then jumped down, overtook the tractor and walked to the water tank. He broke the sheet of ice with the fork and lifted it out with his hands. Then he opened the gate, allowed Nicholas through, closed the gate again and climbed up behind. Nicholas moved to one side and he took his seat to return to the sheds.

Indoors, Helena was preparing breakfast. She took one look at her son and laughed. "You look like a refugee," she told him. "Your nose is blue, there's snow in your hair, your gloves are frozen solid and your knees are bleeding. I'm surprised the blood hasn't frozen too. Did you have a nice time, darling?"

Nicholas' teeth chattered.

"Come here, darling, let me warm you up." She held him to her and rubbed his back vigorously. "You should wear a hat, you know. I'll have to knit you one. Come over here, let me look at your hands. We'll take those jolly old gloves off and put your hands in warm water. Then we'll wash those old knees of yours. I think you could probably do with a change of clothes in fact. Let's get on with it."

Within half an hour, Nicholas was warm again. He was allowed to eat his breakfast off a tray in front of the stove and, on finishing it, he read for most of the morning until Helena switched on the wireless for the request programme for soldiers abroad, which they always listened to on a Sunday.

He wished he did not have to go back to school but realised it was inevitable. He liked school but just wished he could come home at night. This was how it was going to be. School, home; term, holidays; winter, summer; football, cricket. This was how it would be for the next ten years.

TWELVE

The clouds scudded across the sky on a cold August morning. The alarm rang at a quarter to seven and Nicholas leaned over to switch it off. He tipped himself out of bed, stood up and stretched. Work began at seven.

He washed his face but left the rest until later. Stumbling downstairs, he lifted the kettle on to the stove. Helena had made his meals overnight and left them in a tin. He had put in a special request for fried bread and Marmite sandwiches. He added a bottle of squash and placed the food in his bag. He made a cup of tea, drank most of it and went out to the tractor shed.

His appearance caused some amusement. "Look at that, John-boy," Ernie said. "He remind you of them creatures on that programme?"

"Bit too much beer I reckon," John commented. "Slep' in his clothes. Brought his breakfast no doubt." Nicholas realised he was still carrying his teacup. He drained it and set it on a ledge.

"Morning, Ernie. Morning, John. Would've brought you a cup of tea but I forgot. Want me to go back?"

"We're now going. Fifty acres to cart today."

"Fifty!"

"Depending on our fourth man, if he's up to it, mind. Need a strong arm, fourth man."

Bill emerged from behind the tractor, where he had been filling the tank. He burst out laughing when he saw Nicholas. "Reckon he left his hairbrush up that school of his," he told the others. "Come you on." He climbed into the tractor.

Eight years on, the current tractor had a cab to protect against the rain. It did not protect against much else, looking flimsy and impermanent. Bill had his food bag on the floor, took off his coat, laid it on top and made himself comfortable. The other two men climbed on to the trailer. Nicholas stood on the drawbar and held the sides of the tractor. He wore gloves as a protection against the binder twine, the string that held the bales together.

"Been a while since you did this," Bill shouted over the noise of the tractor, changing gear and pulling the throttle out.

"You want me to drive the tractor on the field, Bill?"

"We got to take it in turns. One of us got to get up and help John-boy. He in't as young as he was."

"How old is he?"

"Nobody knows. He got the pension four or five years back. Still kep' on coming to work, never asked him if he wanted to stop. Wants the seven pound ten a week. Reckon he'd stop if he wanted."

"Can't he drive the tractor and we do the loading?"

Bill laughed. "John-boy never driv a tractor, Nick. He can't ride a bike without falling off. They never invented tractors when he started work. We do the best we can. We got all day."

"Are you still catching rabbits, Bill?"

"Nah. None of that. Since myxie no-one eats rabbits. And you don't need to keep them down, they keep themselves down. This time of year they get myxie again." Nicholas was not surprised. Not long after he went away to school, rabbits had begun appearing everywhere with myxomatosis, eyes bulging, feet dragging, bumping into things. At first people killed them out of pity. Later they left them as the task grew overwhelming and the animals did not seem to be suffering. Eventually the numbers of sick animals reduced but still, at this time of year, it would be unusual to go outside without seeing two or three dying slowly.

They reached the field. Straw carting needed at least four men. On a large farm you could have ten men in a gang: two pitchers, two loaders, three tractor drivers and three men on the stack. The pitchers, walking over the field, had the toughest job: a day on the fork was enough for anyone. On a small farm, however, it was a four-man job. No-one could pitch alone, so it was two pitchers, one loader and one driver. If, of course, there was a driver.

The bales were lined in a row across the field. The baler had a sledge on the back where a man caught the bales as they came out of the machine, stacked them in heaps of eight and released them with a trip at the same point on each row of straw. When it went smoothly, the bales stood in a line and the tractor could drive between two heaps. When there were only four men the pitchers would throw one heap across to another one so the tractor did not have to move so often.

Bill drove the tractor for the first load; stopping the tractor by the bales, he got down to help pitch. They filled the trailer and took the load to the corner of the field, near the gateway, and began the stack. Ernie climbed in the tractor to drive the second load.

"Hang you on tight," John-boy said with a twinkle.

"Why's that, John?"

"He reckon he drove a tank in the war. No wonder them Jerries gave up. He never learned to drive a tractor though. Whoop!" The tractor jolted forward as the men on the trailer, sitting on a bale, clung to each other to avoid falling off. Then Ernie drove at speed round the field before pulling up between the bales.

"Easy as pie, this driving," he told them. "You feeling workish, Nick?"

"Always workish, Ernie."

"Pile 'em on then. There's plenty of room upp'ards."

Loading was a skilled job. On the first layer one bale was laid on each side. The second layer mocked the first: one bale across the middle and one lengthways on each side. The third and fourth layers replicated the first and second. As the load went higher the loading grew more difficult. After six layers, staying in place grew precarious for bales and men. Then there was the problem of jumping down. It didn't matter when they were offloading on to the stack but jumping down from load to ground was a job for a young man.

At breakfast they sheltered under the wind behind the growing stack. They drank their tea and opened their sandwiches. John-boy threw most of his away.

"You'll be courting soon, then," Ernie told Nicholas.

"Courting? I don't think so. Bit young."

"Just a bit of slap and tickle then, eh?"

"I'm more interested in cricket." It was not true and they all knew it. He could feel himself colouring as they laughed.

"All these wages you're getting, got to be buying some young lady drinks up the pub. Whadya say to that, John-boy?"

John grunted. "No doubt," he said.

"Who'd you reckon he'd be after?" Ernie carried on. "That Angela down the yard?"

"No doubt."

"Tell you what, you could do worse. She got a look in her eye."

"I don't even know her!"

"Time you were introduced, then."

Bill got up, perhaps to save Nicholas from his fate. "Nine o'clock," he said, and went back to the tractor.

By twelve, Nicholas was flagging. John-boy seemed unperturbed, methodically loading the bales, then throwing them down on the stack, stopping for a drink on the turn-round. The sun grew hot and Nicholas, unlike the others, was not wearing a hat.

"Want a turn on the tractor?" Bill asked after dinner.

"I still can't drive, Bill."

"The hell if I know. I've got one reckons it's a horse, one reckons it's a tank and one can't touch it at all. You could drive when you were eight years old, Nick."

"What's the clutch for?"

"Clutch cancels out all the gears. You take your foot off the clutch, it's in gear again."

"How do I stop it?"

"Foot on the brake there. And take it out of gear with the clutch, do it'll start up again."

"All right. I'll have a go."

He drove round the field as he had always done, foot pressed down on the clutch to bring the tractor to a halt. He was not strong enough to pitch so Bill and Ernie pitched and John-boy loaded slowly on his own. They built up six layers and that was enough for John-boy. He sat down on the load. Bill waved the tractor towards the stack and he and Ernie walked over.

At first it all went smoothly. The tractor went into first gear and Nicholas drove alongside the stack. He pressed down on the clutch. However, the tractor did not stop. The stack was on a slight hill and the tractor and trailer, instead of coming to a halt, gained pace going down the hill. Christ. What did Bill say about stopping it? How did you take it out of gear? What was the brake?

He began to gather pace as he rolled down the hill. "I can't stop!" he yelled. For some reason Bill and Ernie laughed. John-boy was on top of the load and Nicholas was terrified he would fall off.

He swung the trailer round, like a dodgem, and started climbing the hill again. He brought the load beside the stack and pressed down on the clutch and the tractor came to a halt.

Then it started moving again. It was running backwards downhill.

"Foot on the brake!" Bill cried.

There was another pedal and it had to be the brake. Nicholas shoved his foot down and the tractor juddered to an abrasive halt.

"Take your foot off the clutch. Leave the other foot on the brake."

He did. Another jolt as the engine cut out and the tractor stayed in gear.

When it was clear that the tractor would not start again and the load not roll downhill, Nicholas climbed down and looked anxiously upwards at John-boy. "I'm so sorry, John," he said.

"Fucking thing," John said. "Fucking machine. They never ought to have brung it out in the first place. Fuck did they expect? Fucking machines."

THIRTEEN

It was a cup match. The league season finished at the end of July because harvest started then, but some cup matches remained. Welbeck were playing West Morden in the Callaby Cup.

At teatime Nicholas dragged himself home from work. Helena met him at the door. "They want you to play cricket tonight," she said. "For Welbeck. At West Morden. They're short of players. At half past six. Terry's playing too."

"Christ. I'm worn out, Mum."

"So are the rest of them, probably. Go on, you'd better have some Weetabix and get in the bath. Peter Wright is picking you up at six."

Nicholas was doing quite well at cricket at school; his cover drive was the envy of many and he was developing a useful googly. He had an idea, though, that these might be less than useful in a twenty-over match in the semi-dark.

"Christ," he said again.

Peter Wright arrived punctually at six. He owned a very old, black Austin. In it he had Graham Gardener, known as Goosy. "All right,

99

young Nick?" he said. "You going to help us out? Climb you in the back, then."

Nicholas did so. "Thanks for the lift," he said. "Will we get there in time?"

"Have to. Or they have to wait. I got the ball."

Nicholas laughed. "Do you always have the ball?"

"We owe them one. Our ball got lost in the river when we played them down here in the league. I got a special one here. New ball. Help the swing if we bowl first. If we bat first we take some of the shine off in the motor."

"Are they a good side, West Morden?"

Peter and Goosie exchanged glances. "Wha'?" said Goosie, who seldom said anything else. "Wha', Peter?"

"They don't reckon on us too much," Peter said. "Generally they beat us. They won the league. They got an umpire."

"He cheats?"

"You reckon he cheats, Goosie?"

"Wha'?" They both laughed.

"Yes, I reckon he cheats."

Peter and Goosie worked on different farms, larger than Bill's farm and already well into harvest, but harvesting had finished for the night so that they could play cricket. They reached West Morden at 6.25 in gathering gloom.

The captains, Trevor Taylor of Welbeck and Ben Prior of West Morden, tossed. It was said that the Morden umpire, Barney Basham, had a double headed coin but Trevor made sure the captains tossed alone. He won the toss and chose to bat. It meant they had to bat against a new ball but it also meant that they batted in daylight.

Trevor returned to the area under a tree where they had their kit. "Young Nicholas," he said. "Best you open the batting."

"Me? Are you sure?"

"See the shine off. Bit of classical batting. No need to hurry."

"I'm only sixteen!"

"Never you mind. If you're good enough you're old enough."

Nicholas thought he detected some knowing looks among the players. As if to confirm this, Peter came over to him with some sage words while he was padding up.

"Don't you pay no mind to their opening bowler," he advised. "Saggy Nockolds. He get a bit fired up. Keep you on coming forward. Only one over and he's finished. Works in the brewery, Saggy. Shifts them barrels around all day. Drinks the beer in the bargain. Bit nippy for five minutes, that's his lot."

It was becoming clear to Nicholas that there was no competition to bat number one. Trevor Taylor joined him to open but put himself firmly at number two. "I'll look after this end," he said. "Their second bowler, he's mine. You just keep coming forward to Saggy."

They went out and Nicholas took guard. There were no sightscreens and an oak tree stood behind the bowler. Nicholas could see very little. He was not sure, in fact, when the match would begin as no signal came from the umpire, Barney Basham. However, he could hear something moving fast and breathing heavily at the other end and after a while he guessed it was the bowler running in. He was, however, completely invisible. Suddenly a huge, gasping figure emerged from behind the umpire, hurtled from right to left towards the wicket and flung himself down the pitch. Nicholas was aghast. Where was the ball?

Then he heard a sound above him like a small aeroplane taking off. It was the ball, which he never saw. It seemed, however, to have whistled by some distance over his head. It also cleared the wicketkeeper's head, bounced once on its way to the boundary and finished in the long grass.

With extreme reluctance the umpire signalled four byes. He did not consider the notion of a no-ball or a wide.

"Keep you coming forward, young Nick," Peter called from the boundary. This seemed like the most likely way to get killed. However, Nicholas could only assume, correctly as it turned out, that Peter had local knowledge which had not been shared with him. He resolved to play forward.

As the bowler returned to his mark and ran in again, events at the far end of the pitch became clearer. Saggy Nockolds ran in immediately behind the umpire so that he was completely invisible to the batsman. At the last minute he swerved out to one side of the umpire, who was standing back, swerved back again in front of the umpire to obscure his view and hurled the ball down the wicket as fast as he could. At first sight it might appear that he had no idea where the ball was going. The next few balls undermined this theory.

Nicholas played forward to the first one. The ball landed in front of him and exploded like a firework into his chest.

Trevor Taylor came down the wicket sympathetically. "Don't let them know you're hurt," he said.

"It didn't hurt, actually."

"Next time it will do. Don't let them know you're hurt."

The next ball landed in the same place, with the same electrifying effect. Again it didn't hurt. Nicholas went to examine the wicket, perhaps to pat down the spot where the ball had landed. It was an impossible task. The pitch was mottled green and brown and resembled the surface of the moon. The ball might have landed anywhere.

The fourth ball was identical. Nicholas, knowing what was coming, managed to approximate its flight path with his bat. The effect was startling. The ball flew from the shoulder of the bat and passed comfortably over the slips, apparently gaining in height and velocity as it progressed. A fielder stood on the third man boundary and the ball cleared his head by several feet for a six.

The umpire signalled a four.

Consternation broke out on all sides of the field. "You're a fucking cheating bastard, Barney Basham," the Welbeck players chorused at him from the boundary. Trevor Taylor went over to him. "You're a fucking cheating bastard, Barney Basham," he told him. "And if you don't change your signal I'm going to lay this bat over your head."

The embarrassment proved too great even for the West Morden players. "Umpire," called third man whom the ball had passed over. "I believe that maybe just cleared the ropes."

"Not from here it didn't," Basham replied. "And there aren't any ropes. Four runs, scorer."

The game took a while to settle after that. Then Saggy Nockolds, refreshed by the delay, came in and hurled the next ball at the identical spot in front of Nicholas' forward defensive shot. This time the ball reared like a spitting cobra and hit him with a dull thud over the heart. He collapsed in stunned agony and rolled over on the pitch gasping for breath.

"Don't let them know you're hurt," Trevor Taylor told him.

Nicholas picked himself up, collapsed again then rose once more unsteadily to his feet.

"Don't you worry about the next one," the West Morden wicketkeeper told him fraternally. "It's a wide. Sixth ball's always a wide. You done all right, young'un."

Nockolds came in at a much reduced pace and bowled a ball which went six feet wide of the stumps. "Over," called the umpire.

"That was a fuckin" wide," Trevor Taylor remonstrated with him. "We got another ball."

The umpire marched off to square leg and the next over began.

Trevor, a good cricketer, hit two fours in the first three balls. Then he hit one to the fielder on the square leg boundary. There was an easy single, perhaps two runs. Nicholas started running.

"Get back!" Trevor called. By this time, however, Nicholas was three quarters of the way down the wicket. He looked up in dismay, came to a halt then looked again. By this time the fielder had gathered the ball and, seeing the position of the two batsmen, had plenty of time to lob the ball back to the bowler's end. Trevor was nailed to the crease at his end. Nicholas began running swiftly back. He had no chance, however, and was run out by two yards. The Welbeck umpire had to give him out.

Crestfallenly, Nicholas made his way back to the boundary. He had let them down. However, he found himself greeted with delight by the other players. "Well done, you young'un," cried Peter and Goosie. "That fuckin' showed 'em. Cheating bastards. Eight off the first over, should have been ten, eleven if you count the wide. Don't you worry about that run out. Not your fault." Not for one moment had Nicholas thought it was his fault. "Trevor only wanted to keep you down that end, seeing as you played Saggy so well."

He realised that Trevor had declined the single because he had no intention of ever facing Saggy Nockolds.

This was confirmed by Terry, who came over laughing to greet him. "All right, Nick?" he asked. "Last time it were me. They put the young'uns in to face Saggy. It's only for one over. Trevor's only making sure, in case Saggy takes a second. But he won't."

And he didn't. Saggy Nockolds retreated to the outfield, breathing in racking gasps, and took no further significant part in the match. Welbeck, having been given a fine start, scored 108 in their twenty overs and won the match by 37 runs. They were helped by the complete darkness which enveloped the West Morden innings.

Afterwards in the pub, Nicholas was plied with drinks and showed off his bruises. Officially he and Terry were drinking shandy, but the men bought them pints of mild. They sat near the dartboard and listened to the delighted laughter of the players as they celebrated victory. By the time he reached home at eleven, Nicholas could hardly stand.

Fourteen

"There's an invitation to the hall for tomorrow," Helena told him.

"The hall? For us?"

"Just for you. I've got to see someone in London. I might stay the night. I hope you don't mind. I thought you were probably old enough to be on your own now for a night."

"Blimey. I might starve to death."

She was not sure if he was joking. "I'll leave you plenty of food."

"Who's going to find me if I starve? If I have a brain haemorrhage?"

"The same person who finds me if I have a brain haemorrhage when you're not here."

"No-one."

"That's right. But you're not going to starve any more than I am. Do you mind if I abandon you for one night? I'll leave a telephone number of course."

"Of course not, Mum. It'll be a bit strange though."

"And you'll probably be at the hall till late. Take a torch. You'll have to walk back."

"Do I have to go? Why have they invited me? And at the last minute? They've never invited me before."

"Oh, I don't know." She was vague.

Helena cooked a large meal for Nicholas that night and cooked lunch for the next day. Leftovers could be put in the oven in case there was not enough food at the hall. She drove off in the afternoon to leave her car at the station overnight. In London she belonged to a women's club, set up for modern professional women in an attempt to match the gentlemen's clubs in St James's. The women's club was in Bloomsbury. She told Nicholas to ring there in case of any crisis and they could contact her. In any event she would telephone him when she arrived.

"What are you going to do in London?"

"Oh, I've got to see a few people. An audition, a read-through, an interview for a newspaper." Again she was a little evasive.

Then he was at home on his own. Terry came round after tea. Terry had already left school. It seemed incredible to Nicholas, for whom school was part of the encircling world, something that would go on for ever, that Terry was finished with it for good. Terry had started work on the hall farm. He was a man!

"Hello!" he exclaimed at the door. He could never restrain his delight at seeing Terry, unmanly though it seemed.

"Are y'all right?"

"Come in. Want some grub? I've got leftovers."

"No, I had tea. Your mum not here then?"

"She's in London for the night."

"You're on your own? You could have a party. Get some girls in."

"I don't know any girls."

"That's true. Still, I could round a few up."

"I'm off to the hall tonight." He showed Terry the invitation. "To Helena and Nicholas. At home."

"Jesus, Nick. Mixing with the toffs now or what?"

"They've never asked me before."

"Your mum hin't never been on TV before though, have she?"

"Christ." It had never occurred to Nicholas. "You think that's why they've asked me?"

"Wouldn't surprise me. Mix with the famous."

Helena was playing on television in a serialisation of Great Expectations. While she had been occupied solely in the theatre her profession had not influenced Nicholas' life at all. Even when she began making films, most people did not see her on the screen in her succession of mid-market British dramas. However, television was different. Every home now owned a set. Everyone watched it. Nicholas never saw television at school but on the first evening of the holidays he rushed to the Radio Times to see what was on. Holidays meant television.

Wrapped up in the pleasure of it, though, like a hard stone in the middle of a peach, was his mother's acting career. People might see her now and know who she was. Furthermore, they might know she was his mother.

"Bloody hell, Terry."

"Don't let it put you in a bad mind, though. Go there, eat their food, drink their drink, come home."

"You want to come?"

"They never invited me, Nick. I only work for them. And I got to be up early anyhow. Feed the cattle first thing."

"I can't believe you've left school, Terry. Working already."

"Couple of years on the farm, then I'm going in the forces. Army with a bit of luck. Otherwise air force. Learn to be a fitter. See the world."

Nicholas felt both lucky and unlucky. Unlucky that he could not go out and face experiences like Terry's at a comparable age. Lucky that he did not have to. At school he read about wars and politics and poverty and sex. He only read about them, though. He often thought about the soldiers, all over the world, who one week were playing football, the next week were getting shot. Was that going to happen to Terry? More likely, he hoped, he would just go on playing football. Wars didn't happen any more, and that was the way you wanted it. Terry would join the army and see the world.

"So when are you off to the hall, then?"

"I think it's eight o'clock." He looked at the invitation. "It says 7.30 for 8.00. What does that mean?"

"Buggered if I know, Nick. Your friends not mine." He laughed. "Reckon you better get there about quarter to. Split the difference."

"Maybe."

"And get a clean pair of pants on. Never know, might get lucky." They both howled.

ele

At 7.45 lights shone all over the big house. Nicholas climbed the stairs to the entrance and was about to push the bell when the door opened, apparently by instinct.

Inside stood an employee of some sort, butler or waiter or simply hired hand. "Good evening, sir," he said.

"I've been invited," Nicholas told him. "I've got my invitation here."

"Please go through. You may wish to leave your coat on the left."

Nicholas did so. Did he need to remove valuables? Actually he hadn't got any. Even the coat was worthless. He left it and proceeded up more stairs. At the top stood a woman whom he could only assume to be Mrs Spencer, wife of the Colonel. She was resplendent in a large blue dress with a prominent yellow brooch and a turquoise necklace. The texture of her skin reflected an outdoor life and a cold house.

"Why, hello," she said. "How nice that you could come. And you are?"

"He's Nicholas Hutton," another voice interrupted. It was unclear where the voice came from. A number of girls and young women stood nearby. Behind them was Colonel Spencer, who clearly had no idea of the identity of his latest guest.

"I'm very sorry that my mother couldn't come tonight," Nicholas said politely. "I'm afraid she had an urgent engagement in London."

He was aware that he was being inspected from all sides. He could think of no more to say.

"He's Nicholas Hutton," the voice said again. Then its owner stepped forward: a tall, thin, bony young woman with red hair and blue eyes. "Do you remember me, Nicholas?" she asked him. "I'm Millie. I came to your house when my mother was in hospital that time." She turned to her mother. "Nicholas Hutton, Mum. His mother is Helena Manning."

"Oh, dear boy," Mrs Spencer told him. "Could your mother not come tonight?"

It was hard to know whether he should repeat what he had said before. He was saved from making a decision when Millie took his hand. "Come with me and get a drink," she suggested. "It's much easier to deal with my parents after a good drink."

The main hall was long and high and cavernous. Ancient squires looked down from their portraits on the walls. The current landed gentry stood at intervals along the barely carpeted floor. At one end of the hall was a table of drinks, or at least of poor quality champagne and unidentified whisky. To one side a crate of beer had been introduced for any employees who were invited. Millie thrust a glass of champagne in Nicholas' hand. "I've already had five," she confided. "Got to get through this bloody affair somehow. How old are you, Nicholas? I'm nineteen."

"I'm sixteen. You were eleven last time I saw you."

"And a precocious little brat too, I expect. I had a lovely time playing with you and your friend Terry. I often wanted to come back. You're very good-looking now, Nicholas, aren't you? Drink your champagne."

He complied. He had no answer to any of her other remarks. He drank another glass. Millie seemed to have gone. He could see no-one else he knew. At the opposite end of the hall from the drinks was the food. He headed for it. The hall was thick with people and travelling from one end of the company to the other took time. He reckoned that if he went to the food, ate his share, came back to the drinks and drank another glass of champagne he might be able to go home. No congenial way of prolonging this agony presented itself. He held his glass of champagne in one hand, reached the food and piled bread and lettuce on his plate. He didn't like the look of the rest.

"Would you like a tour of the house?" Millie appeared at his side again.

"You've changed since you were eleven," he said.

"Yes. I was short and fat. Now I'm long and thin. I'm still the same inside, though. Come on round the house. Leave the food, it's disgusting. Bring the champagne."

They went out through a side door into a stone corridor. Millie led the way up a bare staircase to another door. Beyond it was a corridor with carpets. Bedrooms stood on either side.

"I got to university eventually," Millie said. "Not in this country, they wouldn't have me here because I hadn't got any education. I'm at Geneva doing French and philosophy. You're still at school, I suppose."

"I've got another year after this one. It seems like an age."

"My God, I should think so. This is my bedroom. Want to come in?"

He was given little choice. The bedroom was capacious and dimly lit. A dresser and a full length mirror stood in the corners and Nicholas could see a bed, covered in cushions, cats and old dolls. "Wait there a minute while I go to the lavatory," Millie said. "Sit on the bed."

Nicholas made space for himself and sat, nervously sipping his drink. In a very short time Millie returned. She turfed the cats out and sat beside him.

"This is nice," she said.

"Yes."

Then she put her hands on his shoulders and began kissing him. Nicholas had kissed a few girls before and was not intimidated. However, she then sat on his lap, facing him, put her hands under his shirt and started kissing all round his face and neck. She took his hands and guided them to her breasts. The effect on him was instantaneous. He knew she must be able to feel him, hard against his trousers.

"This is very nice," she confirmed. Then she took her dress off over her head. She unhooked her bra and moved his hands under it, enclosing her small, smooth breasts. He had never felt a naked nipple before. "Oh, that's good," she told him. She pushed him back across the bed and lay on top of him, kissing his chest, licking his shoulders and neck. "Oh, Nicholas," she said. "Oh, Nicholas. Please take your clothes off. And mine."

He began to undress. Wanting to laugh, he remembered Terry telling him to wear a clean pair of pants. He was too slow, however, for Millie. Within moments she had pulled off his trousers and pants. He had never felt so naked. She moved his hands to her and he removed her petticoat and knickers. Suddenly shy, she climbed under the covers and pulled him with her. He found himself half on top of her and, his leg between hers, he realised she was wet.

"Your finger," she told him.

He moved it to her, felt her wetness. Moved his finger up and down.

"Put it in me," she said.

She had to guide him until his finger was right inside her. Then deeper. She moved backwards and forwards, clearly indicating that his finger should do the same. He pushed it in and out. Then suddenly she removed his hand and pulled him on top of her, parting her legs. She moved her hand down and held his penis, startling him almost beyond recall. She guided him to her again and said "push". Within moments he was half inside her. He pushed again and he was right inside her. My God, my God, was all he could think. She wrapped her legs suddenly around him, her feet meeting behind, and threw herself up towards him. He had no control over himself and pushed and came and pushed again, silently. She felt him come and arched herself up to him, continuing after he had finished, pushing more and more. Noises came from her, small cries, and her body shook all over. Then she lay back underneath him and wrapped her arms behind his neck.

"Was that all right for you?" she asked, almost matter of fact.

What could he say? "Amazing," he told her. "Amazing. Thank you."

She laughed. "Thank you too. Was that your first time?"

"Er, yes. I think so."

"I've taken your virginity. I'm so glad. It was amazing for me too. You're very virile, Nicholas. I bet you could do it again now."

It felt as if he could.

"But we'll have to get back, I suppose. It was lovely. We'll have to do it again some time."

He laughed. Then they both laughed, with the consequence that he emerged from her. "Oh dear," she said. "Never mind. I must go to the bathroom anyway." She was gone, with a towel wrapped around her. A couple of minutes later she re-appeared, smiling. "It's the second door on the left," she said.

Nicholas went to the bathroom. He used the lavatory and thought he ought to wash a bit. He found himself smiling all the while. Wearing Millie's dressing gown he returned to her bedroom to find her already fully dressed. She removed the dressing gown from him and stood against him, clothed against his nakedness. She put her arms round him and kissed him on the lips.

"Not a word about this," she said. "To anyone. Please."

"Of course not. Never."

"I'll see you again."

"That's great."

"I'll let you make your own way down. We shouldn't go down together."

"Yeah."

She was gone. A few minutes later he followed quietly. He carried his glass, drained it on the way down and re-filled it in the main hall. He found his plate, untouched, and ate his bread and lettuce. All the rest of the food seemed to have been eaten.

Millie was nowhere to be seen. He recognised a few other people now but could find no reason for them to speak to him and nothing he wanted to say to them. In some circumstances this might have embarrassed him but in the context of the evening he found it insignificant. After a while he slipped out, found his coat and went home.

It was another seven years before he saw Millie again.

For a few days, he thought she would call at the house, or ring, or write him a letter. He sat at the window to watch the gate. Then he realised she was not going to make any contact at all. He hoped she would not forget him. He would not forget her.

After this, Nicholas found that sexual intercourse was a great boost to self-confidence. In addition, he never worried again about having nothing to say in a strange social gathering. He always thought something might turn up.

FIFTEEN

"Well, look who it is!" said Mrs Goodbody as she opened the door. "Body, it's young Nicholas come to see you. Only he's not so young now. Bit like a giraffe, he's got to bend down to get in the doorway. Nicholas, it don't seem long since you couldn't touch the top."

"Come in, Nicholas," called Mr Goodbody. "It's getting so I don't get up if I don't have to. You come to watch the cricket, then? Come you on in, we shall watch it together. It's getting a bit exciting, I'm afraid."

Helena, like the rest of the village, had a television now. However, Nicholas knew that Mr Goodbody would like the company. He went on through to the parlour where the couple had been drinking tea and watching the test match. "Sit you down while I bring you a bun," Mrs Goodbody told him. "Go and talk to old Body. Don't let him tell you all them old stories again. It's right nice to see you, Nicholas. Saw your mum the other day on TV but we hin't seen you for a bit."

"I'm sorry about that, Mrs Goodbody."

"Never you mind about that. I'll be in in a minute."

Mr Goodbody was more frail than he used to be but not as frail as he pretended. Nicholas knew for a fact that he did his garden, chopped wood, rode his bike and went for walks in the woods that had been his life. He still had a twinkle in his eye, too. "What say we give them Aussies another hammering, eh, Nicholas?"

They sat down together. Now that her husband had company, Mrs Goodbody did not stay in the room but went back to the kitchen where she could be heard clattering gently about, taking things from the oven and making tea.

It was the fourth test match and Mr Goodbody was happy. "We're going to win," he told Nicholas. "That Ted Dexter, that Lord Ted, he's hitting them all over the ground. Look at that! Did you ever see an off drive like that? Walter Hammond, he could do that, so they say. Lord Ted, though, he's a master. You not working today, Nicholas?"

"They're combining. They don't want me for that. I can't drive on the road yet so they don't want me on a tractor."

"I did hear as how you weren't an expert on driving that tractor," Mr Goodbody said mischievously.

Nicholas laughed. "That's true too," he acknowledged.

"Oh my good God!"

"He's out."

"That Benaud's got him. For 76 . Clever little sod that Benaud, excusing my French. See where he's bowling? Into the rough. Well, Ted's gone but there's plenty to follow. Peter May next, he's better than Dexter, he got 95 in the first innings. We'll soon sort them out."

Peter May followed, bowled round his legs, sweeping, for nought. "Oh my sainted aunt!"

There was a terrible pause in which Nicholas and Mr Goodbody stared at each other, stunned and open mouthed.

"What got into him? Bowled round his legs, sweeping, to a leg spinner, against the spin and into the rough? What got into him, Nicholas?"

"I don't know, Mr Goodbody. Peter May, of all people."

Brian Close came after Peter May. Brian Close, the hardened battle warrior, the man of all England for a crisis.

Unfortunately he appeared to have gone completely mad. Left-handed, he too tried to sweep every ball, this time with the spin. He missed them all. Then he hit a ball straight and it went for six. The crowd - and several million television spectators - roared and thought he had seen sense. Play straight. Don't go mad. But he reverted to sweeping. He missed everything. Nicholas thought Mr Goodbody might chew his cup to pieces. Finally Close connected with a sweep. The ball flew up in the air and was caught by Norman O'Neill at square leg. Close was out too.

"The hell if I know. They must've put something in the tea. What's possessed them? Dear oh me." England needed 256 to win but were now 158-4. "The hell if I know. What's happened, young Nicholas?"

"I don't know, Mr Goodbody. Twenty minutes ago I thought we were going to win. Now I think we're going to lose."

"I never seen the like. There's been times we got beat. 1921 when they had Gregory and McDonald. 1948 with Lindwall, Miller and Bradman. Both of them was after we had wars, made a difference. This time we had the game won. Dear oh me."

Mrs Goodbody came in. "Don't tell me we're losing now," she said. "We were winning just a minute ago. What you done to them, Body?"

"I never done nothing, mother. They give themselves away. Blast me."

"Oy. None of that language in here. And in front of young Nicholas. What'll his mother say, he larn language like that?"

"I dare say he heard worse. Anyhow, what do you expect, losing like this when we had it won?"

"Them Australians," she said. "All that sun."

"Eh?"

"It's no wonder. All that sun. You remember Ted Parnell? He thingummy, emigrated to Australia. Flo got a letter back. Reckoned the sun shone all the time. It's no wonder."

Mr Goodbody worried at his moustache and burrowed further and further into his armchair. "They want a good smack," he said from time to time. "Whoops, there goes another one. Oh, my giddy aunt fanny."

"Body," said his wife, "you'll do yourself a mischief, you mark my words."

"Now just hang you on, mother, hang on a jiff. We just lost the Ashes for pity's sake."

"Well, they'll have to get some more, then. At least it's only Australia, we've kept it in the empire. What about if we lost to them Russians?"

Mr Goodbody ignored this. "Nicholas, when do we play them again?"

"I think it's next year in Australia."

"They better pull themselves together by then. And that Richie Benaud, they want to send him off on a boomerang somewhere."

Nicholas laughed. "They come back again though, boomerangs, don't they?"

"Well, a whatsit, then, a billabong whatever. Swagbag. One of them things."

They ate their buns and lapsed into silence.

John-boy died as he had lived, not fully sober. He was biking home from the pub when he had a heart attack. The doctor said it was instant. For once it was not the beer that caused him to fall off his bike, but death. A motorist found him, tried to pick him up but had to leave him and go for help. John was all over the road.

"Went how he would have wanted," Ernie said. "Drunk. Poor old sod."

They were standing round in the village hall after the service. Bill was too upset to say much. Nicholas was silent. Helena talked to people, circulated round family and friends. The village had turned out in force. The list of mourners would be in the paper a few days later. Tea was poured and drunk. Sandwiches had been prepared by the women who looked after the hall. They had made buns. Helena had baked a cake. John had two children and four grandchildren. They all looked baffled.

It was hard to understand. Only a few days earlier John had been working on the harvest. (No-one raised the subject but everyone was relieved that they had got the harvest in before he died.) Nicholas had sat next to him against a straw stack. They had talked about off cutters. John was not old, or didn't seem old. Then again, he seemed as old as the hills.

"Look at it this way," Ernie said. "You could have killed him on the trailer with your driving. He was lucky he lived so long."

Nicholas laughed. "You reckon it was close, Ernie?"

"Not far off. Your driving'd kill most people with the shock alone."

John's wife was approaching.

"What's her name?" Nicholas asked.

"Betty. Or That Old Witch. But don't you call her neither if you value your goolies."

"Thank you for coming," the widow said to both of them.

"Very sorry for your loss," Ernie told her. "He was a good old boy, was John."

"One of the best," Nicholas said. It was a phrase he had read; unacquainted with death, he knew no appropriate words. "He was the best loader in the world," he added unimaginatively. "My mother and I are both very sorry, Mrs Fosdyke."

"You must be Nicholas Hutton," she told him.

"Yes, I am."

"John told about you. He reckoned you'd never make a farm worker if there was straw coming out of your arse. He reckoned you were like a girl from London."

Nicholas laughed again. He could see John-boy saying it. His widow moved on to the next group.

"Don't you pay her no mind," Ernie said. "No fuckin' wonder John-boy went down the pub every night. Need to be drunk to come home to that."

Bill joined them. "And how about when he lost his hat?" he asked. The two men laughed.

"What was that?"

"Well, few years back," Ernie began. "Friday night. John-boy got his pay packet. Went home, gave his missis her keep, same as always. Then he goes down the pub. Only first he has to buy a razor, so he takes that in the pub an' all. Time he leaves, half past ten, playing crib he lost his whole pay packet and his new razor. Then he goes and loses his hat!"

"No!" Nicholas had never seen John-boy without his hat.

"Next morning, he comes to work wearing some yellow bonnet his kiddie bought up the seaside. Christ, we near as died." He and Bill were convulsed again.

"How long did he work for you, Bill?" Nicholas asked.

"He worked for my old chap first. When they came back from the first war. When my old chap died they let me have the tenancy and he stayed on after the second war. Forty-odd years all told I dare say."

"Christ."

Lily came over. "Now, then, you lot, what are you all laughing at over here? Don't you know it's a funeral?" She smiled at them all.

"Remember that time John-boy lost his hat?"

She laughed too. "I saw that yellow thing. Thought it was an ice cream man."

"Who's going to coach me at cricket?" Nicholas asked. "No-one's got John-boy's experience, have they?"

"Now just hold you hard one minute," Ernie said. "Several of us got the knowledge. Maybe not got John-boy's experience. Need six pints of brown and mild every night for that. And fifty years straw carting. But Bill and me, we had our day. We had our moments. You should have seen Bill before he calmed down, before the war he was like a wild man." They all laughed.

Mr and Mrs Goodbody came to join them. "Hello again, young Nicholas," Mr Goodbody said. "Bill, Ernie. You've lost your head man, Bill, is that right?"

"Did you know John very well?" Nicholas asked. "What was he like when he was young?"

"We were boys together, John and me. He was a lovely boy. Full of fun. Never a dull moment. We had the run of the place in them days. There were no motor cars, you know. We went out in the morning, they never saw us till night. Out in the woods, catch rabbits and maybe pheasants but don't you tell anyone. Build a fire and cooked the rabbits. Came home when it was dark. And he was a good cricketer too, specially before the first war."

"He told us he was the terror of nine parishes."

Mr Goodbody laughed. "Well, John-boy always told a good tale. I'm not sure about terror. He was a good cricketer though. I used to field leg slip to him. Caught him a good few wickets. I knew his mum too. She was a good old girl."

"Did his dad play cricket too?"

"I never knew his dad. He died of lockjaw, so I believe. Put a pitchfork through his foot and it turned nasty."

"Christ. John never told us that."

"No. I don't believe he would."

Later, Nicholas and Helena walked home. "I can't believe he won't be there," he said. "I was working with him only a few days ago. Will Bill get someone else for the farm?"

"I don't know. I expect so."

That night, in the privacy of his bedroom, Nicholas wept for John-boy.

Sixteen

Willie Dodger was not in the same house as Nicholas at school. However, as a friend of Nicholas from prep school he was accepted as an honorary member of Hallows House, and he often visited at weekends. Nicholas had discovered to his surprise that he himself was popular in the house. He could think of no particular reason for this, but the effect was that he could get away with having a friend over.

Within Hallows, he shared a study with Pringle, the rebel of the house. Nicholas called Willie by his first name, and this was reciprocated. With Pringle, however, and with all other members of the house, it was surnames only.

The three of them were drinking Marmite in the tiny two-person study. Elvis Presley was playing on the record player.

"Wish this was a gin and tonic," Pringle said. "I could do with getting blotto this afternoon. Nothing to do, nowhere to go, only you two chaps to talk to. Fate worse than death."

"You wouldn't know a gin and tonic if it ran up and bit you on the nose," Nicholas told him. "All mouth you are. When did you last have a gin and tonic?"

"Last night."

"What?"

"I don't believe you," Willie said. "Bloody liar, Pringle."

"Want me to show you?" From under his chair Pringle produced a quarter bottle of gin and two small bottles of tonic, one of them half empty.

"Jesus Christ."

"You'll get us all expelled, Pringle."

"Don't worry about that. I'll take the rap. I'll say you know nothing about it. I'd love to get expelled, anyway. Get me out of this bloody awful public school. Go to the local grammar. I passed the Eleven Plus. I could go there any time. I don't believe in private education."

"So you mentioned. Every time you open your mouth. But what are you going to do about it?"

Willie broke in. "And what's the matter with private education?" he demanded. "We're saving the country money, aren't we? They don't have to pay to educate us, we do it ourselves. And we come top in all the Cambridge exams. It's the best education."

"It probably is. Not surprising, when you think of what we get here. Small classes, plenty of teachers, lots of books, lock us up to do prep every day. But all schools ought to have all that. It's like private medicine. When they set up the Health Service they should have made private health illegal. Then you'd get a decent health service. Same with education. Private schools ought to be illegal. When we get in, things'll be different."

"We? Who's we? You a commie or something?" Willie asked.

"We in the Labour Party. When we get back in. Ten years of misrule it's been. The men at the top all went to Eton or somewhere. There's no real people in there. They don't know how the world works for the man in the street."

"And you do?" Nicholas asked.

Willie was beside himself. "I never heard such a bloody load of crap," he expostulated. "Here we are, because our parents worked hard to send us here, made sacrifices, and we're the future leaders of the country."

"We are? In this pathetic little school? You're joking, Dodger."

"When we get in again at the next election," Willie said, "we're going to do the job properly. All those nationalised industries - the Coal Board, British Railways, the Electricity Board, the Water Board - we're going to make them all private again."

"The Water Board's never been private. You must be mad."

"Who's we?" Nicholas asked.

"Us. The Conservative Party. I'm going to be an M.P. Put this country back where it belongs. Like the USA. There'll be private health care again for everyone as well. You've got to give people incentives. Let them work hard. Cut taxes. Pay for what they use."

"And the poor? The sick? People in wheelchairs?"

"Anyway," Nicholas interrupted, "you'll be back in Cut Bank, Montana, Willie, you won't be a Conservative M.P. You'll be on a hoss, rounding up steers."

"It might be my duty to stay. To put this country right. The American way."

"Jesus Christ, Dodger. The only good thing to come out of America is Rock and Roll. And that was invented by your slaves. You want to go back there as soon as you can. We don't want you here."

"But I'm a football referee. They don't play football in the U.S. I've got to stay."

The tension was broken as they all laughed.

"The first thing to do," Pringle said, "is to get out of here."

"Of the school?"

"Here. Everything. Get On The Road." Pringle had been reading Kerouac. "Get away from this closed-up society, our parents, our Sunday lunches, our church bloody services, our public bloody schools, all that crap. We need to see the world, go to London, Paris, meet James Baldwin, the beatniks, visit Rome, Athens - all those places."

Nicholas had seen Pringle's copy of On The Road but neither he nor Willie knew anything of this James Baldwin. He did, however, have a very good idea of why Pringle wanted to go to Paris. It had, he thought, less to do with James Baldwin than with Brigitte Bardot.

There was nothing like it. A goal, a beautiful, humming, soaring goal.

The ball left his foot like an intercontinental missile. It speared the air and shimmered past the goalie's flailing arms, exploding into the netting. Everyone stood and stared, rooted, mesmerised. Then the applause started.

Life, for Nicholas, could never be so sweet again.

He hoped it would be, though. He hoped that both cricket and sex could be as sweet as this football moment, although it seemed unlikely. He turned back towards the half way line. It was not good form to demonstrate jubilation. Within the school, in fact, it was a punishable offence; when, over lunch, their housemaster had been asked why, he told them that we did not build an empire through showing our feelings. In matches against other schools, however, it was considered patriotic at extreme moments to support one's colleagues. A handshake was in order before trotting back to the half way line. Nicholas hated shaking hands. All the hands he shook, at football or elsewhere, seemed to be clammy, sweaty and limp. He could imagine where the hands had been. What he really wanted after scoring a school was to turn a coruscating cartwheel. However, it would get him expelled. And he couldn't turn a cartwheel anyway.

When he was eleven, Nicholas had planned to play both cricket and football for England, like Willie Watson, Arthur Milton and Denis Compton (only wartime internationals in Compton's case). By the time he was sixteen he knew he was not good enough at either sport. It came as a blow. However, he retained hope of playing one or the other at first class level. Cricket would be favourite.

It was a football playing school, thank God, not a rugger bugger. The thought of getting his head kicked in every week by a pack of brainless wonders made Nicholas feel ill. There was a future in football. Most of the school football team thought no further than playing for the school or perhaps their university. They didn't even go to watch professional football. They thought footballers were lower class: which, of course, they were. Nicholas loved football. He watched village matches, pub teams and other school teams. In 1958-9 he had followed Norwich City avidly as they, a lowly third division side, progressed to the Cup semi-finals, knocking out Manchester United, Tottenham Hotspur, Sheffield United and Cardiff en route. They were the greatest Norfolk heroes since Nelson.

Before he went back to school Nicholas went with Terry and Bill to the United match. On a snow covered pitch, totally unfit for play, Norwich won 3-0. Less than a year after half the United team had perished in the Munich air crash, it seemed a bit like shooting a deer. Nevertheless, it was the greatest day of their lives.

Nicholas knew he was not naturally talented: not by real standards. He was not even good enough for the school team if natural ability was the only yardstick. However, he worked hard. He tried to enlist Pringle to help him with training but Pringle declared himself an aesthete not an athlete and declined his support. Willie Dodger, however, though too scared to play himself, was happy to assist between refereeing duties. He planned and supervised an endless series of twenty yard dashes, weight lifting, ball skills with either foot, tackling, heading and passing. Nicholas twisted and turned in the penalty area, shot from a distance and close in, sprinted back to the half way line, beat the full back on the outside and crossed. On the practice pitch he was supreme.

Training, of course, was deeply unfashionable and showed signs of dedication. Most of the rest of the team were keen to share their opinion of his unseemly activities. "At it again, Hutton? Practising your swerve?" "Going to be the new Stanley Matthews, are you?" "Haven't you got a home to go to?" Nicholas didn't care. He became fitter than any of the others in the first team squad, and tougher too. He fought his way into the team, to the resentment of many.

For the rest of his life he would remember that goal. He knew he would. He wanted to write home to Helena about it immediately. He wanted to tell the newspaper. He thought he should be made captain of the school. He didn't want to be captain of the school or anything else in the hierarchy but he thought they should do it anyway.

He remembered a brilliant catch he had taken at cricket in the summer. That was a rival moment. Both occasions were better than sex, as far as he could tell so far. They had an added advantage over sex as well: you didn't have to spend all evening talking to a girl.

At teatime, in the house, it was "Well played, Hutton! Smashing goal, Hutton!" He was actually applauded into the dining room. It was embarrassing, even though he felt like applauding himself. These were the same people who had derided him for his training and practice, for the hard work that had overcome his lack of higher ability. He remembered; he wondered if they did.

Pringle was another matter, of course.

"Here, Hutton. I believe you triumphed in some sporting occasion, is that right?"

"I scored a goal, Pringle. A great goal. It won us the match against our hated rivals from Ipswich. As you know."

"Hated? I don't hate them. They are my comrades. I only hate the prime minister and the headmaster."

"Good for you, Pringle. But I hate them. They're from Suffolk."

"Anyway, you're a hero, is that right?"

"So they say."

"I'm pleased for you. Want a gin and tonic?"

"No! God, Pringle, I can't get expelled on the day I'm a hero."

"Nor you can. What a pity."

"And football is a working class sport, Pringle. You ought to be playing. How do you get out of it, anyway?"

"I have a little known complaint called Housemaid's Knee. It is brought on by playing football. Housemaids get it in winter. Probably through playing football."

"Did you catch it off a housemaid?"

"Regrettably, no. It's genetic. Generations of Pringles have borne it. It prevented my great grandfather, a career soldier, from serving in the war in the Sudan."

"That must have been tough for him. Aren't you worried about your body going into decline at sixteen? When you're twenty you're going to be a big fat blob. You'll be dead at twenty five."

"When I'm twenty, Hutton, I shall be athletic. I may take up mountaineering or channel swimming, something that pits me only against myself. I am not prepared to participate in the privileged jingoism of school sports. I am quite prepared to come with you to watch Norwich City, especially if we're supposed to be on the school premises at the time. Then when I'm eighteen I can do what I want athletically. But not because the bloody establishment tells me to."

"It was a great goal though, Pringle."

"I'm very happy for you. But it doesn't compare with the struggle in Cuba or Algeria."

"That's true, Pringle. It doesn't compare at all. I bet they'd much rather have scored that goal than get independence, though."

Seventeen

Dear Frances,

It was lovely to see you the other day and I wish it had been for longer. We ought to go away somewhere for the weekend together, just you and me. We always seem so rushed otherwise.

As you know, I am in this new series on TV that's coming out in the spring. It seems to be going quite well so far. The director, John Phillips, is very good and most of the cast are friendly. Unfortunately my co-star (if I can use such a self-indulgent word) is a bit of a nuisance. You know who it is. He spends all his time in rehearsals looking in the mirror and keeps telling me I'm upstaging him. He forgets that we're not actually on a stage and that there are cameras all round. Perhaps he means that I act better than he does. Well, I'm afraid that that may be the case. C'est la vie, old sport.

Nicholas is coming on in leaps and bounds. He writes every Sunday even though he doesn't have to. He comes home on every day out. We have a good talk in the car and he tells me about football, English, his friends and his views on politics. He shares a study with a communist. Then I give him a big lunch and he goes out looking for his friend Terry, if he's around (Terry spends a lot of his spare time chasing girls now) or helping Bill if he's working, or just wandering around the farm buildings. He loves it here and I still, after all these years, feel guilty when I take him back to school. I hope I haven't done him irreparable harm.

I think I hinted to you that I have a new admirer. He has been here a few times when Nicholas isn't here. I try to keep it that way. It's a very difficult situation, I'm afraid, where a mother has a new husband, or just friend. You know what it was like after the Great War when there was a generation of women without men. It's happened after the Second War, too. Many of the men, if they came back, had been away for years. Others, like Hugh, didn't come back at all. If the mothers find a new husband, the children just don't know them and they don't like them taking their mothers. Sometimes it works, sometimes it doesn't. I'm just not sure I want to take the risk with Nicholas. Even at sixteen he's still a child.

When Hugh died I was an ice maiden for a long time. Since then, as you know, I have had admirers but I have been very, very discreet. I don't think Nicholas knows about any of it. But I do like men, Frances, and I do really like - I can say this to you and to no-one else on earth - I really, really like having a man in bed with me. Burn this letter! I suppose I am only saying what we all know. We quite like sex.

Let's change the subject! Have you read A Woman In Berlin, by an anonymous author? It's a shocking account of events after the Russians entered Berlin. I came across it the other day and was appalled.

I've been reading a variety of authors. I'm afraid I'm always on the lookout for a book that could be filmed, although most of the good ones seem to have been taken already. Anyway, my choice of authors has been quite wide recently. On the one hand I've been reading good old Nancy Mitford, who I must say is hilarious; I've met her a couple of times at dinner and she's very good value. Graham Greene goes from strength to strength; The Quiet American is an extremely good book. John Masters for simple adventure: I love him. On the other hand, I've been through all the kitchen sink stuff, as we have to nowadays. I do really like Alan Sillitoe; what a good film, too, with Albert in the lead. Finally I have to admit that I've been reading some of Nicholas' books. Have you tried the Tolkien? It really is terrific and I just couldn't put it down. I gave him the T.H. White recently, too, The Once And Future King. Very, very good stuff.

I'm out tonight for dinner at the Hall. I'm afraid they have really taken an interest in me since I've been on the telly a lot. Ah well, it's an opportunity to see how the other half live. I can tell you it will be freezing cold, the potatoes will be soggy and the meat won't be cooked. They may even have forgotten I'm coming. But there'll be whisky for pudding and I can listen to talk of stalking in Scotland and the price of timber. It's best to stay off politics; these people always assume you agree with them and, if you demur ever so slightly about hanging homosexuals and vegetarians, they look at you as if you've taken a turn.

Then I can walk back in my big coat in the dark, stoke up the fire and go to bed with a book. London again tomorrow to talk about shooting. (That's not shooting as in shooting pheasants and homosexuals, but shooting as in television.) Until we see each other, then, lots of love.

Helena

—ele—

Dear Nicholas,

Thank you so much for your letter. I do look forward to getting them on a Monday. I'm sorry I'm a day late in replying. I had to go to London today, Monday, and only started writing on the train coming back. It was no good, though, trying to write on the train. Some people seem to be able to do it but when I try it all comes out wonky. I'm sitting at home now in front of the fire with a glass of sherry and a piece of toast. If you were here I would cook a proper meal, of course, but I can't always be bothered when I'm alone. I had lunch in a restaurant today so that will have to do.

By the way, I had another letter today as well as yours: from Miles and Hubert. Well, from Hubert, actually. He seems always to want to keep in touch with me, perhaps because we were at Cambridge together. Those were his best days, I think. I never told you all about Hubert and perhaps I shouldn't now, but he did always like playing the female parts in revue. I'm not sure whether it was the dresses or whether he just liked the excuse to be, well, feminine. Anyway, he was rather well known for his preferences.

Did you know that Hubert was friendly with Guy Burgess, who ran away to Moscow? I knew Burgess slightly too. When he and Maclean defected we were all interviewed, even though it was sixteen years later. In Guy's papers they found an invitation from Hubert to a party in 1935. I think I was there too. You never knew you had a commie sympathiser for a mum, did you?

With what the Americans are doing to Cuba I could be a commie sympathiser again. They seem to think they can control everyone, everywhere, and if they don't like a country they just think they'll invade it.

I went up to London to talk about another television series on BBC. They have got a good part for a middle aged, middle class woman. Just at the moment, these parts are like gold: everyone is young and working class unless they're Edith Evans. Unfortunately I'm middle aged now and there's no arguing with my middle classness. (Is that a word?) It was more than an audition today because I think I've already got the part, but it was a chat about how to do it. They seemed to like me, anyway. So you may have to hide behind the sofa again because your mother's on TV. I promise not to tell anyone at school!

I had lunch with my friend Peter Dennison today. You will have to meet him some time. I'm having dinner with him next week when I go up again for the night.

Very glad to hear about your football. You do seem to write more about football than Chaucer. I wonder why that is?! Your marks seem very good, anyway, and if you really can do your A levels in one year it would be marvellous. I would be very proud of you and probably tell all my friends how clever my son is, so they'll all hate both of us.

Looking forward very much to the weekend. I'll pick you up at the same time, same place.

All my love,

Mum

P.S. Bill says he's always got some muck carting to do at weekends....

EIGHTEEN

It was not an exeat weekend but there was no school match that afternoon and they were supposed to be working or practising football. Nicholas and Pringle were reading James Bond and Mickey Spillane.

"Hutton, does your mother work?" Pringle asked suddenly.

"Not really, no."

"Was your father rich, then?"

"He was comfortably off."

"And I suppose she gets widow's pension, all that." Pringle knew about these things. Nicholas let it lie.

"Inherited wealth too, I dare say."

There was no television at school and, even if there were, it was unlikely that any of the boys would recognise Nicholas' mother. He took elaborate pains to keep her identity secret. The thought of the whole school seeing his mother on TV was mortifying.

"We're going to do away with all that, of course."

"Yours too? Your inherited wealth?"

"And did you know the public schools get charitable status? The state is subsidising them. That's you and me."

"I'm subsidising myself?"

"Speaking figuratively, of course. It's all completely wrong. If they paid tax properly the fees would be double and no-one could afford them."

"You could, Pringle. Your parents are rich."

They were interrupted by a knock on the door. Willie Dodger came in. He gestured at their cups of tea. "Thought you'd be on the gin and tonic by now," he said to Pringle.

"Bit early for me, old boy. You can have some though, if you like."

"Good God, no. You'll finish up an alcoholic, Pringle."

"I do hope so. What brings you here, Dodger, apart from a concern for my welfare?"

"Nicholas, what are you doing this afternoon?"

"Same as this morning, probably. Reading James Bond. I might practise my superb goalscoring skills."

"Fancy going to a real match?"

"What real match?"

"Norwich are at home. We could leave here after lunch and get back for supper. There's a train leaving at 1.40. We could just catch it if we run. Then there's a train back ten minutes after the match finishes. We could run back here from the station and be in time for supper. No-one would know."

"Christ, Willie. We could be seen going to the station. Or on the train. And I haven't got any money." Cash was never needed at school.

"I've got some money. I could lend it to you. We could go down the back path to the station. No-one goes that way. We could say we're going to the Shed if anyone sees us. That's near the station." The Shed was the acronym for the School House Education Dept, a farflung classroom.

"We could get expelled for being out of bounds."

"Your father was a war hero," Pringle pointed out. "They're not going to expel you. You'd probably lose an exeat. You might get a beating, I suppose. Three strokes or six, depending on the Old Fascist's mood."

"Christ." Beating was very, very painful. The Old Fascist was another acronym: Oliver Freeman was a bilious headmaster with a vicious cane.

"Do you want to come, Pringle?"

"To a football match? Maybe one day, but not this time. I suppose I could go to the pub instead."

"It's up to you then, Nicholas."

Nicholas was not by nature a rebel or a rule-breaker and he did not like taking risks: particularly not risks that might involve a severe caning. He looked at them both. They looked at him.

"All right," he said.

Lunch was cottage pie and cabbage, followed by apple crumble and custard. Nicholas was aware that he had to run hard for ten minutes afterwards for the train, but in any event he was too nervous to eat much. As the meal ended at 1.30 he was out of the door, grabbing his mackintosh to cover his school blazer. At the back path he found Willie already waiting. They ran together, in step, for seven minutes; everyone knew how long it took to reach the station. People were standing on the platform; the line was often deserted during the week but Saturday was a busy day. There was no queue at the ticket office, however, and Willie bought two day returns to Norwich. The train came in on time and they found seats.

"What happens if it's late coming back?"

"It won't be. It starts at Norwich. It's got to be on time."

"Christ, Willie, if we're late back we're in big trouble."

"Don't worry, Nick. Just enjoy the football."

It was a mystery how Willie, conformist in all things, scared by almost everyone and everything, could bunk off the school premises with insouciance. How would Willie explain it to his parents if he was expelled? How would Nicholas explain it to Helena? He looked round at the other passengers, half of whom were going to the match, noisy and exuberant, waving their green and yellow scarves, some twirling rattles, singing "On The Ball, City". None of them appeared to have a care in the world. None faced a ritualistic caning when they got home. All were happy to support their team.

From Norwich station it was a short walk to the ground. They ran: anyone wanting a quiet stroll to the ground in plenty of time had caught an earlier train. They reached the turnstiles at the River

End, the end closer to the station, joined the queue and went in. The match was just starting.

It was tumultuous. The whole, open stand was like a sea on a rocky shore, whole waves of spectators flowing towards the bottom when there was excitement, then ebbing back towards the top when it died down. The pitch itself could barely be seen through the crowd but Willie caught a glimpse of the Norwich goalie, Sandy Kennon, down below them.

"We're going down the other end," he said.

"What?"

"We're attacking the other end. We want to be at that end if we score. We'll come back at half time. We'll be attacking this end in the second half."

"Willie, you must be mad."

"I've got my spot down the other end, in the Barclay. Six steps back from the lefthand goalpost. All my friends'll be there." He set off.

There was no choice but to follow. The noise and the crush were incredible. They moved up to the back, trying to look over the top of the crowd whenever a large roar went up. The River End stand ran continuously into the South Stand, which in turn ran into the Barclay at the other end. They edged their way round the back. At times, when there were obstructions, they had to burrow down a few rows then burrow up again to the gangway at the back. The crowd was tolerant of their journey but it was hard going. Eventually they arrived at the Barclay stand, level with the left hand goalpost, just as a massive eruption of sound washed totally over them. Norwich had scored!

Willie grabbed Nicholas by the sleeve and dived into the crowd. Instantaneously they found themselves several rows further down as the mass of bodies swept them towards the pitch. The ecstasy died slowly and the crowd moved back up, cheering, waving and laughing. The boys stayed where they were and allowed the mob to sweep back past them. Already they were half way down the stand. Over the next five or ten minutes, Willie drove his way down to his regular spot.

"Who scored?" Nicolas yelled at him.

"Dunno." He turned to someone else. "Who scored?"

"Allcock." Terry Allcock, recovered from his broken ankle the previous year, was coming back to his best.

"Header," the informant added.

Willie found his rightful position in the stand and looked round at his match day friends.

"All right?"

"Are y'all right?"

That was the sum of the conversation. Soon it was half time.

"We'll go back the other end," Willie said.

"Bloody hell, Willie, we've only just got here."

"It's easier at half time. We want to be there if City score again. And we've got to be at that end to catch the train."

Half time lasted only ten minutes. They had barely reached the River End, standing this time at the back, when the second half started.

Nicholas loved all this. At least in theory he loved it. He loved the inferno of noise, the singing, the joy of the crowd, the passion of the football as Norwich pushed harder and harder for a second goal. It never came. Towards the end of the match the crowd was aware of the danger of conceding a goal, of throwing away the lead and a priceless point. In the last two or three minutes whistles shrilled all round the ground as the spectators commanded the referee to end the match. Finally he did. A high, extended blast signalled two points to Norwich.

As the whistle blew, Willie grabbed Nicholas' arm and they battered their way to the steps. They ran down, round the spectators already departing, reached the bottom and set off for the station.

Thorpe station was thronging with Saturday traffic, passengers coming and going in all directions. The Yarmouth train, the Lynn train, the Wells train, the London train, all of them stood waiting. They reached theirs with two minutes to spare.

"Cup of tea, Nick?"

"Christ, yes. I'm parched. I'll pay you back when I've had an exeat. Get some money off Mum."

"If we're not expelled."

"Bloody hell, Willie, I don't know how you can do this. I couldn't do it again. If we get away with this, I'm never setting foot outside the grounds on a Saturday again."

"Good, though, wasn't it?"

"It was marvellous."

Their train left Norwich on time but, despite Willie's protestations that it never happened, it was delayed en route. They arrived five minutes late.

They ran back to school faster than on the way out. At the back path they separated. Nicholas ran in the door to his house just as the boys were going in to the dining room. He tossed his coat on the floor of the boot room.

"Don't put that there, Hutton!" a prefect yelled at him.

"Sorry, Ashman. I was afraid I'd be late. Permission to put it in my study?"

"Leave it there. You're all sweaty. Where have you been?"

"I was in the library."

"I bet you were. See me afterwards. Get in there now."

He had got away with it. He knew he had got away with it. He sat down on the bench beside Pringle.

"Good book in the library, Hutton? Found a new work of Chaucer criticism?"

"Very good, Pringle. I'd recommend it. It was very perceptive."

"Glad to hear it. Even made you sweat. I bet it was some sex book you found in there."

General laughter rippled round the table.

NINETEEN

Nicholas turned in off the road, through the trees and into the long sweep of the gravelled drive. He had walked from the station. Ahead lay the old school, towered and turreted, red and green, tall and square. The sight of the building brought back overwhelming memories. This is ridiculous, he thought, it's only three years since I left. Anyway, I wasn't happy here. I wanted to be at home. How can I be nostalgic?

"Dear boy!" exclaimed Miles, answering the front door himself. "How very handsome you have become. We have been looking forward so much to your visit. Come in, come in. Have you walked from the station?"

"Yes. It only took about half an hour."

"Good boy. Independence of spirit. We like an independent boy. Now come in and tell us about that horrid uncivilised public school of yours and everything else you have been doing."

He was shown into the drawing room, where senior boys had been given sherry on a Sunday after church. Tea was brought by one of the house staff, a woman from the village called Maureen who recognised him immediately.

"Why, it's Nicholas!" she cried. "Nicholas Hutton. Oh, I'm very sorry, I don't want to embarrass you but I must just give you a big kiss." She put her hands on his shoulders and kissed him on the cheek. "Well, look how big you are. I always had such a soft spot for you, Nicholas. If you're ever wanting a wife just let me know and I'll set you up with my daughter Elizabeth. Do you remember Elizabeth?"

"Of course I do, Maureen. She used to come in on Sundays and play in the kitchen. She came down and looked at my stamp albums once."

"I bet she'd like to look at your stamp albums now. Anyway, I mustn't keep you talking. Sorry, Miles, only I just had to speak to Nicholas. Lovely to see you, Nicholas."

"And you too, Maureen. Really lovely. Perhaps I can pop down to see you later?"

"You do that."

Miles was amused but made no comment. Hubert came in extravagantly, swishing a scarf round his neck. "Ah, Nicholas, you're here. Very good letters you write. Full of pungent wit."

"And no commas," Nicholas pointed out to Miles. "The first draft of my last letter had six commas in it. They sneaked in. When I read it through I had to sit down and write a fresh letter."

"Quite right."

They poured tea and drank.

151

"So how is that school of yours?" Miles asked. "We may send other boys there. Inside information would be pertinent. Is it barbaric? Is it totally devoid of culture? Do they beat you and make you take cold showers?"

"It's all right most of the time. I'd rather be at the grammar school at home, to be honest."

"You always did like your home. And your mother. And the farm, I seem to remember."

"The cricket's good. The football's not bad. They play rugby but I try to avoid that. Willie Dodger's becoming a football referee."

"Willie Dodger! That poor little mouse! Among all those tigers! Something painful must have come over Willie."

"He was too frightened to play so he became a referee. When we have games on a Saturday he goes out to the town and refs in the local leagues. He gets his expenses paid."

"Good Lord. What expenses?"

"Oh, whistles and things. Clothes for refereeing in. Fares. Cigarettes."

"Cigarettes?"

"They're not allowed to give him cash apart from expenses so they give him cigarettes. He sells them to someone at school."

"Perhaps the less we know about that the better. How about the work?"

"English is good. We've got a good master for A-level. History's not too bad. They want me to do Latin A-level."

"Ah, a classical scholar."

"I'm useless at it. They think because I did well at O-level I can do A-level. Because I'm doing badly at A-level they think I'm messing about. Willie's doing History too. But he's going into politics, he says."

"Politics, dear?" Hubert said it as if it was gynaecology or Farsi.

"He says he's on the right wing of the Conservative Party."

"Oh, the dear boy. Well, he does come from cowboy stock."

"I'm thinking of being a socialist."

"A socialist? Not a beatnik or a homosexual?" He pronounced it "hommosexual".

"Or a road manager," Hubert intervened. "Everyone wants to be a road manager, we understand. For pop stars. It's very fashionable."

"I was a socialist once," Miles said.

"No you weren't, you were a communist," Hubert told him.

"Ah, that was for form's sake, you had to be a communist because of Spain. I was a socialist after that. I think I still am, probably." He sipped his tea and lit an elegant Turkish cigarette.

"Really? I wasn't sure you'd like me being a socialist."

"Of course, dear boy, you must be a socialist. Everyone should do it at least once in their life, preferably but not necessarily in their youth. After that, you should see what suits you best. If you're rich it might be a good idea to be a Conservative."

"We have big debates about it at school. Willie and this chap Pringle. He's a rich socialist."

"Ah, the dear boy."

"Can I come back and see you more often, Miles?"

"Of course you can, you big puss. You should come back three times a year. You can tell us about socialism. And English. You said in your letter that you are going to read James Baldwin. That's good. And Angus Wilson you should try; he's a chum of ours. And Olivia Manning."

"My mother reads Angus Wilson."

"How is Helena? You should bring her with you. It would be glorious to see her again."

"She's very busy. She's in these things on TV now."

"We know. We watch her without fail. She looks lovely. Just the same as in 1935."

"I'll tell her you said so. How's the school? Is it going well?" He asked almost with trepidation, afraid that he might be told that the school was collapsing, that there were no more pupils, that he would turn into the drive and nothing would be there.

"We seem to be doing rather well, dear boy. We're rather popular and quite full. Can't think why. But it pays for our little trips to Glyndebourne and Venice, you know. We have a rude collection of boys compared with your day, of course, but they are still polite when compared with hoi polloi. Some of them are passably intelligent and we have a good violinist and one half-decent cricketer."

They talked. Then Nicholas went to see Maureen. It was four hours later when he left to walk to his train.

TWENTY

Terry came round after work.

"Had a hard day then, Nick? Slaving here in the warm? All that book work?"

"Piss off, Terry."

"Cup of tea, Terry?" Helena asked.

"Please, Mrs Hutton. I came round to ask Nick if he fancied a spot of mucking out tomorrow. Bill's on a day out."

"Bill? A day out? I didn't know he ever had a day out."

"They can't take no more beet in for two days so Bill and his missis, they're visiting his sister. Ernie's feeding the cattle only they need a couple of boxes mucked out. Bill sent me round."

Terry had taken John-boy's place on the farm. After leaving school he had worked here and there, principally at the Hall, but when John-boy died Bill had asked him to come. He did not need a second offer. Working for Bill was like being at home, he said, only more fun.

It was strange to think of working on the farm without John-boy being present. Nicholas had never worked without him. When he was home from school he still helped feed the cattle on Sunday mornings and he still went over every weekday morning with a cup of coffee for them if they were in the sheds. The balance of relationships had changed, though. Formerly, Bill, Ernie and John-boy had been the men and he had been the child. Now Terry was there and he was a man. At the same time he was Nicholas' friend and he was a boy. He took some of Bill's attention. Nicholas was not the only son. It would be strange to work alone with Terry, whom he knew he might come to resent.

"When are you going in the air force?" he asked. "How old do you have to be?"

"I can go in straight off. Got to see Bill right, course. Can't leave him short. Get through harvest and that."

Harvest was eight months away.

"And maybe the harvest after."

A year and eight months.

"You won't never go," Nicholas told him. "You're frit of leaving, Terry. Here for good. Fifty years on the farm."

"Nah! I got to see the world. Get out of here. Get a trade."

"But you're getting a trade," Helena said. "You're becoming a farm worker."

"Yeah, but it hin't a real trade, is it?"

"Of course it is. And it's valuable. Where would we be without farmers? Where would we be without food? We could manage without an air force, Terry, but not without food."

There was silence for a moment.

"You been reading them books of Nick's, Mrs Hutton," Terry said after a while. "Them ban the bomb things or what? Saw them on your kitchen table."

They all laughed. "They aren't my magazines," Nicholas said. "They're more like my mum's. On some things she's one of them."

"Buggered if I know. 'Scuse me, Mrs H. Pardon my French. Took me by surprise a bit."

"You can still go in the air force if you want, Terry. But I think farm work's more useful. So you'd better take Nicholas for a day mucking out and show him what's best for him. And you."

Mucking out started at seven.

At this time of year it was dark, very dark, for at least half an hour after seven o'clock. Nicholas took a torch round to the sheds. At home he had had two cups of tea, nothing else. It was cold out. Snow was forecast, earlier than usual; generally it was new year before the days grew longer but the frosts came sharper and the snow billowed in. Nicholas had on four layers of clothing. He was well aware that he had been privileged through working on the farm only in summer and for occasional unloading of sugar beet in winter. The real work took place in tough, bleak conditions.

"Morning, Nick. You laid behind or what?"

"I'm only one minute late, Terry."

"Fucked if it in't sharp this morning. My balls nearly dropped off waiting for you."

"I'm too cold to notice. Too cold to know it's cold."

"Soon get you warmed up on that muck. You got your boots?"

"Sure."

They fetched two four-tine forks, two shovels and a brush and Terry reversed the two-wheel trailer into the cattle yard. He was driving tractors now; he was not allowed to take them on the road but he could drive round the farm buildings and on tracks. A four-wheel trailer was still beyond his expertise because it was impossible to reverse, but he backed the two-wheeler up to a box and let down the back panel.

Two boxes had been cleared of cattle and allocated as their task for the day. They were deep and compacted with muck, straw and oozing liquid. The boys began at the door.

Terry took a forkful from the top; it was too deep to lift from the bottom. He turned and threw the compacted muck into the trailer. Nicholas did the same. He was wearing gloves because of the cold and to prevent blisters. Each one got out of the way while the other threw the forkful as far as possible into the trailer. Terry took his next forkful, going down lower. Liquid seeped from the bottom. The smell grew as the top surface was removed. Terry took no notice. Muck-carting, in a warm and fusty atmosphere, was not an unpopular job. By breakfast time they had cleared a quarter of the box.

They washed their hands in the freezing water from the yard tap before having breakfast in the hay shed. By now, Nicholas could feel sweat trickling down his back and sticking to him. He was both boiling and freezing. He chewed on his fried bread and Marmite sandwiches and wondered how he would survive the day.

"You like that school of yours then, Nick? Do it shew you how to get on? Make money and that?"

"I dunno about that. I dunno if I like the school either. This is a lot better than school. But there's things to think about. They get you into university. Play cricket. Then they talk about things. There's this chap Pringle. He's a socialist. They all hate him. He talks a lot. I'm going to his family for New Year. It'll be interesting."

"You can talk a lot here. What's so great about that? You can be a socialist here an' all. I'm a socialist."

"Are you?"

"Course. Everyone's a fuckin' socialist. We're the next government, hin't you heard? Sweep away them old bastards. Wind of change. We're all going to get motors, washing machines, TVs. Go on holidays up Spain. When I get in the air force I'm going round the world."

"You'd get on well with Pringle."

"I don't reckon I would, Nick. He'll probably finish up prime minister, him being a toff. No time for the workers put the food on his plate. Too busy reading about it, Karl Marx and that."

"Do you know about Karl Marx?"

159

"A bit. Give you a surprise, eh? Daily Mirror did a series on him. Then again I reads the New Statesman sometimes, get it off some feller up Lynn on a Saturday when he's finished with it. Prefer the Mirror, mind. Now eat your fuckin' fried bread and Marmite, Nick, we got muck carting to do."

It was two minutes to nine. They finished their food, drank from their flasks and left their bags in the hay shed for later. They drove their load half a mile up the track to the muckheap on the edge of Church Breck. Unloading in a brisk wind was a lot colder than loading up. After half an hour they were pleased to get back to the warm cosiness of their calf box. They had two more loads to fill before dinner and they built them as high as they could go. The higher the loads, the fewer times they had to go out in the cold.

By four o'clock in the afternoon, Nicholas was stiff from the back of his neck to the back of his heels; everything at the front was just fine but his rear had almost entirely seized up. He knew the next day would be worse. It didn't matter how much football you played or how often you went to the gym, real life was different. He thought this was a lesson he should not forget. They left the tractor in the shed and put their tools away and he walked slowly home.

He took his boots off outside the door and left them there. He stepped inside, into the wonderful warm world of the kitchen, smiled at Helena and reached for the teapot.

"Out!"

"What?"

"Out of here! You smell like a sewer!"

He laughed. "I've been muck carting, Mum. What do you expect me to smell like?"

"You take that jacket off and leave it in the shed. Then that jumper goes straight in the machine. And your trousers. Now. Then you can go upstairs and get in the bath and bring the other clothes down afterwards when the first lot has done. Wash your hair. Clean your teeth. Then do it all again. Don't come down again till you smell like a harem."

"Mum, no need to get savage. Can I have a cup of tea?"

"Never mind the "savage". One day with Terry and you're speaking like a village boy again."

"I driv the tractor, Mum. Terry he shew me how, do I darsn't."

She laughed. "Here. Take a cup of tea. Hold it well away from you. Don't put the cup in the bath either. When you come back down you can have some toast."

"Gee, thanks, Mum. What about when they want me tomorrow for more muck carting? More clothes?"

"Do they want you?"

"No. I was just kidding."

"On your way, big boy. Up those stairs."

She was a tyrant sometimes, Helena. She ought to do some mucking out herself one day, he thought. To be an actress you had to experience all sides of life.

TWENTY-ONE

Nicholas was reluctant to allow anyone from school to come to his home. For one thing, his time at home was his own and he did not want anyone imposing on it. For another, he was afraid someone might find out that his mother was on television. An actress. Famous. Everyone in the village knew, of course, and watched her all the time; he could do nothing about that, and anyway, that was people at home. It was another matter for people at school to hear. His life would never be the same. Willie knew but he would keep it to himself. The rest, even the staff, had never recognised Mrs Hutton when she came to the school. He lived in terror of exposure.

Pringle was keen to visit the Hutton homestead, as he put it. He wanted to see simple country folk. However, he did not push the matter. Instead he invited Nicholas to his home for New Year.

The Pringle family lived in Welwyn, in Hertfordshire. (Old Welwyn, as they later pointed out, not to be confused for one moment with Welwyn Garden City.) It seemed a long way off and it meant being away from home during the holidays, and Nicholas was not at all keen. However, he did not know how to refuse. Through

Christmas, a wonderful Christmas as always with all the treats and comforts of home, he put it out of his mind. He ate and drank and opened presents and read books and helped feed the cattle. A few days later, the invitation, long since accepted, could no longer be forgotten. He travelled down on New Year's Eve. They were due to go to a party that night.

What would the Pringle family be like? They hardly ever came up for exeats, which involved an overnight stay for them. When they did come, they always took Pringle to a slap-up French meal at the most expensive restaurant on the Norfolk coast. He said he hated it.

What was Pringle's first name? Helena had told him firmly that he must not call him Pringle when they were at home. Apart from anything else, she laughed, the whole family might respond. They giggled together at the prospect of Mr and Mrs Pringle, Pringle himself and all the little Pringles responding to the call of "Pringle!"

Actually he did know Pringle's first name. It was James. It seemed a ridiculous name. However, first names had been so drilled out of the whole school population that it was embarrassing even to think of them. In Hallows House they had twin brothers who called each other Johnson major and Johnson minor when at school. Did they do the same at home? Did their mother say, "Pass the salt please, Johnson mi"? Was there a Johnson tertius at home?

Nicholas wished he had the courage to take a revolutionary stand on names. At prep school Miles and all the other teachers had seldom called him by his surname. In the village at home it would have been farcical. Perhaps he should start calling all his fellow pupils by their first names. And the masters? He was overcome with hilarity. Even calling Pringle by his first name would have been dangerously subversive. He was not a rebel, unfortunately. It was easier to go along with the absurdity.

He caught the train from King's Lynn and changed at Cambridge. Helena gave him five pounds, which seemed over-generous. He only had to buy his ticket but Helena said he might need to buy some drinks and perhaps he should buy Mrs Pringle a gift. The rest could go on a book at the station or perhaps a meal somewhere if he was stranded. "In a snowstorm?" he asked. "Or an earthquake? On the way to Hertfordshire?" Just don't worry about it, she said. Take it.

"Hutton!" Pringle cried at the station. "Over here!"

Pringle was standing beside a slick blue car. From the driver's seat emerged a middle aged woman, about forty, in a blue twinset that, surprisingly, did not match the car. Mother and son came on to the platform and Pringle grabbed Nicholas' suitcase.

The boys did not touch in any way. However, Mrs Pringle held out her hand and Nicholas shook it. He had never shaken hands with a woman before. Her hand was soft and small and a little moist. It was such a strange feeling that he would have liked another opportunity to shake it to make sure he had remembered it right; but he never had one.

"We're so pleased to see you," she said. "James has told us so much about you." Had he really? God! "He says you're good at cricket and football but you also read books, unlike the rest of the house." Was this true? Did no-one else read? He had never thought about it.

"Thank you very much for having me. It's very nice of you."

"It's lovely to have you. We're all going out tonight for New Year's Eve. It's a family occasion, a party we're going to. It's a Scotsman so they have haggis."

"Jolly good."

"You won't think that when you taste the haggis. Here, get in the front. James can go in the back, it will do him good."

Nicholas got in where he was told to but had barely settled when the car roared away from the station. By the time they reached the end of the approach road they were travelling at thirty five miles per hour. Mrs Pringle appeared to think she was Stirling Moss, or perhaps his sister Pat. She overtook two cars on the High St and narrowly missed a delivery lorry.

"Steady on, Ma," Pringle said. "Got all day, you know. You nearly killed three old ladies back there."

"What nonsense. Anyway, they should get out of the way. This is a public highway not an old people's home. Silly old bats."

Nicholas gripped the edge of his seat. He realised that he had not really known many drivers. There was his mother, who drove carefully because the car often broke down. There were several people from the village who drove in the way that most Norfolk people drove. Miles and Hubert had driven children around and were liable to be distracted by a tree in bloom or by cloud formations. But none of them drove like this. Perhaps this was what the real world was like.

They entered a quiet street lined with large mock Tudor houses. It would be right to say that they slowed down; or rather, they did not drive quite so fast. A high brick wall concealed the Pringle family home. Beyond it, a narrow gateway led to a gravelled drive. To the sound of squealing from beneath the car, which Nicholas hoped was from the brakes rather than a pedestrian, they scorched through the gateway and came to a halt in a shower of gravel.

"My mother has ruined six gateposts so far," Pringle observed. "But she's got enough money to buy new ones."

"Nonsense, darling, it has been only three as you well know. Now then, where were we? Oh yes, we're home. James, take Nicholas to his room so he can powder his nose. Unpack his case. Then bring him down for tea. Then you can both have your baths before we go out. Nicholas, tomorrow we will show you round the area, perhaps take you to Hatfield House. There isn't time today. When my husband gets home from work he'll have his bath and we'll have a drink and then we'll go out. Now you can go upstairs."

The house was large. A wide staircase led from the hall. Another staircase could be seen down a passage at the back. The hall and stairs were decorated with family portraits and photographs and reproductions of well known paintings. Above the staircase hung a chandelier. A set of antlers loomed over the hall. Bright wallpaper covered every room.

"Come on, Hutton," Pringle said. "Er, Nicholas, I suppose. Come on upstairs. If you stay down here there's a danger you'll meet my terrible sisters. They're a pain."

"How old are they?"

"One's too old, the other's too young. Nineteen and twelve. No use to you. But let me tell you about the girls at the party tonight." He led the way upstairs, turned right and flung open a door. "Over there's the bathroom. This is your bedroom, the guest room. Hope you don't mind, you've got a double bed. Be useful if you bring anyone home tonight."

"Bring anyone home?"

"Only joking. Have to storm the battlements to get anyone in here. And have you ever seen such conspicuous riches as this house? I don't want any of their inherited wealth, by the way. I'm going to make my own way. Work for a living."

"Doesn't your father work for a living?"

"If you call it work. He's a banker. In a private bank. And he was born with a silver spoon, public school and Oxford, all that."

"Like you."

"Haven't got to Oxford yet. Anyway, even going there would be a rebellion. Everyone from our school goes to Cambridge, don't they? Except the thickies, of course."

"Most people, in fact."

"Well, most people are thick. Now, let me tell you, Hutton - Nicholas - about this party tonight. They're friends of my parents. Mother's got a few risqué friends but it's the one night of the year my father lets his hair down. And these people invite all kinds. She's an actress. So there may be some fast girls there. This could be the night we get our end away!"

Oh God. First of all, actresses were clearly beyond the pale, which presumably would include Helena. Second, should he tell Pringle about... his experience? The answer was no, never.

"Where's the party? Is it near here?"

"A few minutes' drive. Out in the country. I tell you, Angela, that's Mrs Montague, who's the actress, she's got a younger sister I've had my eye on for ten years. She's not far off our age, plays the cello and you know what they're like. Bit of a bluestocking as well. All in all, you can't miss."

"Me?" Nicholas had no idea what cellists were like. To his knowledge he had never met a cellist. Not a female one, anyway. Robson, T, played the cello in the school orchestra.

"So you can unpack your case if you want, then come down for a cup of tea. Bottom of the stairs, just shout."

It took Nicholas less than half a minute to unpack his case. What was he supposed to do after that? He lay down on the double bed and closed his eyes. He thought about Millie. If there should be other girls wanting, say, to kiss him tonight, should he be faithful to Millie? He doubted, somehow, whether she would be faithful to him. It wasn't likely, anyway, that other girls would want to kiss him. He could never think of anything to say at parties. It wasn't like school, or home, where you could spend most of the time listening to other people. You were expected to entertain, to be charming, and if you didn't you were boring and didn't get attention from girls.

The whole thing was appalling. It was always like this. The idea of parties was initially irresistible. Then, when you realised you would be exposed yet again as a turgid drone with the sex appeal of an ant, the concept became horrific. He wished he was at home with no expectations. Couldn't he just do some mucking out instead?

He turned out to be Major Pringle. Pringle's father was a tall, dark, smooth man who arrived home each day at six thirty on the dot except when the trains were late, and had a drink with the family before going upstairs for his bath. When they were going out he had two drinks, one before his bath and one after.

"Glad to meet you, old boy," he told Nicholas. "Shocking day at work. Has to be done, I suppose, someone's got to keep the wheels of finance turning. Been taking over a smelter in Western Australia. Godforsaken country, Australia. So you're a friend of James, eh? Hope you'll keep him on the straight and narrow. Got all kinds of pinko ideas in him at the moment."

"Not pinko, Father," Pringle said. "Red. For socialist. For the next government. For the future."

"God forbid, if the future's full of Gaitskell and his crowd. All as bad as each other. Think the world owes them a living. I'll go and have my bath."

"You do, dear," said Mrs Pringle. "Now, Nicholas, another gin and tonic?"

"Yes, please." Nicholas had never had gin and tonic before. At first it shocked him, the flatness of it, the feeling of emptiness. Then he found he liked it. Indeed it seemed to cheer him up quite a lot. He could see why Pringle wanted to smuggle it into the school. Pringle was already on his third tonight, in fact.

The two sisters came in. Diana, the older one, was, as far as Nicholas was a judge, a bit of all right. He didn't understand why Pringle had dismissed her as too old. Certainly she was old, but Millie had been older too. When they got into the car to go to the party he found himself next to her and, as there were four on the back seat, it was pleasurably uncomfortable. Her leg was pressed against him, so was her arm and as they went round a corner he was sure he felt her breast pushing at him. But it may have been something else, perhaps her bicep. He hoped she could not see the effect it was having on him.

The younger sister, Laura, was indeed too young to be interesting.

"Do you come here often?" he said to Diana in the car. Then he could have kicked himself for the cliché. "I mean, are they good friends of yours?"

"Not very. It's just a New Year thing. I don't think they find us very interesting."

"Oh, Di-Di! How can you say that? Angela Montague is a dear friend of mine. And Henry, he's divine, and got pots of money as well. He's on the County Council, did you know that, dear? I think it's rather sweet."

"I know that," said Major Pringle. What it was that he knew was not clear to Nicholas. He was driving. He did not drive as fast or as waywardly as his wife but he believed that other traffic should make way for him. Nicholas wondered if he was better suited to the parade ground than the main road, where others would obey his commands.

Very soon they arrived. It was a large country house in deepest Hertfordshire, surrounded by trees, hedges and lawns. Lights blazed. They parked inside the gate, behind about twenty cars already there, and walked up the drive to the open front door.

"Darlings!" cried Angela Montague, waiting there for them. "So good to see you again! Welcome to our humble bash. Rest assured, you don't have to eat the bloody haggis. Henry insists on having it every year but it's disgusting and I tell everyone not to eat it. And you must be Nicholas? My, you're a handsome brute, aren't you? I'll have to keep my daughter away from you or she'll be tearing your clothes off. In you come. Please help yourselves to drinks over there. There's a punch, there's wine, whisky, take whatever you like."

Nicholas was, he knew, flushed from the feet up. If some girl tore his clothes off she would find a red person underneath. He was particularly worried about the thoughts of Pringle's sister Diana. She must think he was an arrogant beast. He walked across with the others to the drinks room and took a glass of white wine that someone handed him. He didn't really like wine but, like gin, he found it got better as you went on.

In another room food was laid out as a buffet on a large table. He had truly never seen so much food. He took a plate, helped himself and ate. He avoided the dish which held a large notice saying "Haggis. Do not eat". He cleared his plate and filled it again.

After that he was not sure what to do. Pringle had disappeared. So had the sisters and the parents. Nicholas sat on a chair.

Mrs Montague - Angela - came swiftly over to him. "Now, you've not to sit on your own, dear boy," she told him. "God knows, it must be boring staying with those stick-in-the-mud Pringles, you mustn't be bored here too. You may charm me with your wit and erudition. Then I'll introduce you to some lissom young thing and you can charm her too. No sex on the premises, though, only wit and erudition. Am I embarrassing you, dear boy?"

"Oh, not at all. Well, not a huge lot. It's just that I'm not used to beautiful fascinating women being nice to me." The wine, on top of the gin, was beginning to talk.

"Ah, there you are. I knew it was there, you flatterer. Now, tell me about yourself. Still at school, then? And so mature. So, what are your special subjects? Are you a real hotshot on the old Sanskrit verbs or what? Or biology, so you know all about my very personal functions? Are you a budding genius? Classical scholar and all that?"

"They seem to think I'm clever. I prefer cricket and football, though."

"Oh, my dear, muscle and a brain too, how can I contain myself? What about your parents, what do they do?"

"My parents?" Nicholas was never asked about both parents. Strangers only asked after his father's livelihood.

"You know, those people at home. We call them parents. Remember them, dear?"

"My father died in the war."

"Oh, I'm so sorry, darling. What about your mother? Does she have a job?"

"She's a.... well...." For once, Nicholas felt it might not be disadvantageous to have a mother on the stage, so he plunged ahead. "She's a.... well, she's an actress."

"Is she now? What's her name?"

"Well, it's.... She's called Helena Manning."

"Helena! My God! I've known Helena since we were in Miss Gartree's dancing classes together! Good God. I haven't seen her in bloody years but we were in plays together before the war. I gave it all up, you see, when I got married, bloody fool. But she's done so well, carried on where she left off. This is wonderful news. I adore Helena. You must tell her you've met me and you must give me your address and number. I'd love to get in touch again. But, dear boy, meanwhile I must rescue you from those boring, boring Pringles. However did you come to meet them?"

"I'm at school with James. He's not boring. He's a socialist."

"Yes, of course. They'll soon drum that out of him or they'll cut him out of their wills. Old Henry Pringle, he's not very socialist at all, perhaps you've noticed. More of a line-'em-up-against-the-wall-and-shoot-'em sort of chap. Well, this is all very wonderful news. I'm going to introduce you to the most interesting, most beautiful, most charming girl I can find. I shall be insanely jealous, mind you, but I shall pretend she's me. And you can have sex on the premises after all, since it's you. Just don't frighten the horses."

Horses?

Angela Montague drew him by the hand across the crowded room. There stood a dark-haired, slim, beautiful girl with a pointy nose, possibly the same age as Nicholas, talking to a girl and boy who seemed agog in front of her. "Excuse me," Angela said to them both as she drew the dark-haired girl from them. "Hettie, this is Nicholas. Nicholas, this is Hettie . Hettie is beautiful and clever and athletic. She's a bit of a firebrand as well. Hettie, Nicholas is handsome and clever and athletic but he's a bit shy. He needs drawing out. His mother is Helena Manning. Now I'm going to leave you two together. I shall want a report back at the end from both of you." She was gone.

They looked at each other. "My God," Nicholas said eventually.

"Have a drink," she said. She was holding a wine bottle and refilled his glass.

"I'm a bit shy," he said. "Are you really clever and athletic as well as beautiful? And are you called Hettie? Our dog at home is called Hettie."

"Would you like to tickle my tummy?"

"What?"

To his surprise, Hettie lay down, rolled on her back and offered him her tummy. They both laughed immoderately. "Yes," she said. "I am clever and athletic and beautiful. And I really, really like having my tummy tickled. Are you clever and athletic as well as handsome?"

The evening couldn't really go badly after that.

"I'm athletic. They want me to go to Oxford."

"Me too."

"Really? That's amazing."

"What's your subject?"

"English. Yours?"

"English!"

"Wow. What are you reading at the moment?"

"Muriel Spark. Olivia Manning. Elizabeth Taylor."

"Who's she?"

"She's great. What are you reading?"

"Tolkien. Graham Greene. Oh, and Françoise Sagan."

"Sagan? I bet you're the only boy in this room reading Sagan. Can you do the twist?"

"No. Can you teach me?"

"You bet I can. Let's go in there and dance. Then we can talk about books all night."

This party had turned out well but he hoped there was a break in the book talking for a kiss. But qué será, será. She was the only girl he had ever met who could talk about Françoise Sagan. Could she talk about football as well? Or even netball? On the other hand, he didn't really know many girls so maybe they were all like this.

It had been a wonderful night. Major Pringle, having negotiated the route home, turned into the family drive and halted the car. "Fine show," he said obscurely. They all opened their doors and spilled out. Most of them were rather flushed.

Nicholas had talked to Hettie for two hours. He could not, in fact, hear everything she said in the general hubbub, but it was wonderful anyway. She had laughed. She had asked for his address and said she would send him a booklist. He must do the same. They would treat it like a game of snap. Each book must be on a separate sheet of paper. If they turned up the same book at the same time, seventy miles apart, they must shout "snap!". He thought he had kissed her on the mouth. However, in the dark it might have been her ear. In fact he suspected he might not get far with Hettie physically but he would rather be friends anyway. Well, that was rubbish, he would rather have sex with her but he would accept the friendship if he had to.

It had not been the same as with Millie. Millie had given him her body with enthusiasm but her mind remained a mystery. Hettie was the opposite. Was there a happy medium? Perhaps he would never know.

Mrs Pringle had to take out her key to unlock the front door because the major was having trouble finding the keyhole. They all went inside and stood in the front hall, absolutely stationary, for a minute. Then, by mutual consent, they went to their separate rooms. Nicholas did not look up for the light switch. He did not undress. He fell across the bed and went to sleep.

He woke in the middle of the night. The room was spinning. Why was it so dark? Why was he wearing his shoes in bed? Why was he about to be sick?

He rose unsteadily to his feet, found the door and stumbled down the passage. He remembered gratefully where the bathroom was. For a desperate moment he could not find the door handle. Then it turned in his hand and he was inside. Without turning to shut the door he knelt at the lavatory and was massively, revoltingly sick.

It must have been the haggis. No, he hadn't eaten any haggis. Oh God. His stomach heaved like a volcanic eruption. He was sick again and again. It was terrible, it didn't seem to get any better. Was he dying? If he died he hoped there would not be a post mortem. No-one must ever know the cause. He feared he might have drunk too much.

The problem abated and he rose shakily to his feet. He flushed the lavatory. The smell permeated the room and, he was sure, the house and possibly the whole street. He shut the bathroom door behind him and ventured into the passage. Finding his bedroom again was harder than finding the bathroom. Blundering into someone else's room was an outcome he did not want to consider. He decided finally that the one with the open door was probably his. He slipped inside, felt the bed and concluded that no-one was there. He took off all his clothes and climbed under the bedclothes.

A short while later, when he knew he was going to be sick again, Nicholas was faced with difficult choices. One difficult choice. Should he walk naked out of his room and down the passage and, he hoped, just reach the bathroom in time or should he put on some clothes and be sick before he left his room? There was not a correct answer to this question but the decision was inevitable. He left his bedroom without benefit of clothing.

Equally inevitably, Pringle's elder sister Diana was coming out of the bathroom at the same time.

Less probably, however, she was also totally naked. For a wild moment Nicholas wondered whether the whole household went naked after dark. Then Diana explained herself, wordlessly, by turning suddenly and rushing back into the bathroom. She knelt where Nicholas had knelt and vomited from a height into the toilet bowl.

Without any delay Nicholas joined her and they knelt naked, side by side, and were sick together. Their retching came in harmony rather than unison, her sounds a third of an octave below his. Their vomit mingled together in the bowl in a kaleidoscope of whirling colour. She pushed her hair back. He wanted, with altruism so pure that he marvelled at it, to do this for her. However, he was afraid that if he did he might be sick over her.

They finished together and regarded each other gravely. Then Diana rose, swilled out her mouth at the basin and left the room without looking back.

They never spoke afterwards of the incident.

Nicholas was sick only once more in the night. He did not appear for breakfast. He appeared for lunch but did not eat: he had eaten so much at the party, he said, that he had no appetite at all. For supper he ate, with difficulty, a boiled potato. Next day he was very queasy. The day after that he went home. He was fine after that.

TWENTY-TWO

The day before term started again, Nicholas joined Bill and Terry on the farm, taking hay to a farm in Gayton. He should have been revising the Tudors and Stuarts. However, he could imagine no greater joy than sitting on top of a load of hay on a clear winter day, talking to Terry while Bill drove the tractor. The Tudors and Stuarts would wait. They turned left at Gayton mill and followed the main road to farm buildings near the end of the village.

"How's the love life then?" Terry asked, inevitably.

"What love life?"

"Them girls you were having it away with up London."

"Welwyn, Terry. London girls are out of my class."

"No matter where they are. You planning on visiting again? Dirty weekend?"

"Am I hell. Anyway, all this about my love life. What about yours, Terry? Whose heart are you breaking this week?"

"Don't know about breaking hearts. There's Carol Bywater who I see after football on a Saturday. When it's a home game. She keeps me warm at night."

"At night! You mean....?"

"Nah. Course not. More of a coats and bushes job. Or the barn. She's got a good wiggle on her up on them corn sacks I'm telling you."

Nicholas laughed in wonder. And envy. If he told Terry about the Millie incident he would never hear the end of it. They laughed instead at the thought of Carol Bywater and her wiggle.

Bill drove the load into the farm yard and jumped down from the tractor.

"How's your love life then, young Nicholas?"

"Mine! Why does everyone ask about mine? What about Terry's?"

"Never you mind about Terry's love life. We hear about his near every morning. You never did hear such a lot of old squit. Him and that Valerie Beeston. Or Mary Turner. The hell if I know."

"And Carol Bywater, I heard."

"Her and all? Buggered if I know where he gets the energy. Why he's such a lazy beggar in the day I expect." They all laughed. Terry worked like three men.

They unloaded the hay, leaving one bale on the trailer to sit on while Bill drove them home. It was twelve o'clock. Nicholas had brought his dinner with him but he thought he would make a flask of tea while they were back. He strolled across the yard to the house.

Outside the garage stood a green Ford saloon. Helena had said she was expecting a visit from an actor she was about to work with on television. She was so well known now that she had been asked to do a showcase presentation of scenes from Shakespeare on a Sunday night. The other actor, Peter Dennison, was in three of the scenes and he was visiting for a read through.

Not wanting to disturb them, Nicholas opened the back door quietly, entered the kitchen and lifted the kettle on to the stove. While the kettle boiled he opened the hall door to say a quick hello.

A cry, muted but fierce, reached him from upstairs. It was his mother's voice.

It was a cry of pain. Nicholas was momentarily stunned. He had met Dennison and he seemed a decent sort. What was happening?

Another cry followed, and another. Nicholas ran to the sitting room and took the poker from the hearth. Returning to the hall, he paused for a moment. Could they be acting, rehearsing for a Shakespearian murder? But, if so, why were they upstairs?

He was about to call out, to ask his mother if she was all right. Then he thought he should creep up the stairs. But the stairs always creaked. He should run up. Run up and bash the bastard.

Another cry floated downstairs, this time a high, held tone, almost a groan. Then, weirdly, came a noise from the man, a groan too, and another one. The sounds came together.

And then Nicholas understood.

He returned quietly to the kitchen. The kettle was boiling. If she felt it, hot, she would know he had been there. He quickly filled his flask and replenished the kettle with cold water. He slipped out of the back door.

Was that what people did? Those noises? His mother?

He knew she had admirers and these things must happen. But how would he face her tonight? He would talk of normal things, or try to, a book or the farm or going back to school. He hoped he did not see Peter Dennison.

He rejoined the others.

"All right, Nick? That was quick."

"Didn't take long. Just filled the flask. You both want some?"

"Don't mind if I do. You all right? Look a bit pale."

"I'm fine. What's on the telly tonight?"

"Dunno. Your mum in anything?"

"I don't know. She never tells me what she's doing."

Dear Nicholas,

Are you really going to do your A levels in one year? You pretentious beast! They wouldn't let girls do that sort of thing. They'd think it would go to our heads. Also, of course, it might stop us doing domestic science and wanting to take our rightful place in society, at the kitchen sink. By the way, what about all these kitchen sink dramas that are in the cinema now? The last thing I want to see is the kitchen sink when I go to the films. I want an adventure and love and beautiful scenery. Not gritty northern towns. Don't get me wrong, I'm not a snob but there is only so much reality a girl can take.

On the subject of knowing one's place, would you believe that some girls, when they leave here, will be going to finishing school in Switzerland? In the second half of the twentieth century? When I leave here I'd like a starting school, please, not a finishing school. How am I going to handle Oxford (if I get in) when I don't know how to handle myself?

There is so much to learn. I know that all the boys at Oxford (except you, of course) will be trying to seduce me. I have to learn how to handle that - and work - and play hockey - and join societies - and do a real job in the vacations. Perhaps I should start with the job. I need to learn something about the world. My family are wonderful but I don't kid myself that life in Herts is real life: or that it will equip me for university. Oh, it's all so frustrating!

Anyway, on your recommendation I read Kerouac. Mmmm.... What about the women, Nicholas? Yes, it's very attractive for the men, hobo-ing around America. But who cooks the pancakes? Who fries the grits or whatever these people do? I enjoyed Steinbeck more. The Grapes Of Wrath. "A Great Book." You should read Thomas Wolfe and Faulkner, if you haven't already. Closer to home, I've been reading Muriel Spark, who is good fun. Also, a real life-changing book, The Second Sex by Simone de Beauvoir. You absolutely must read this book!

I am playing centre half for the school hockey team. Some people - not me, of course - would say that I play there because I'm the fittest member of the team. (Others would say it's because I'm a bully. Can you believe that?) We have lost only one match out of six so far this term. I want to keep playing hockey when I get to university. It would be great to get a blue, but I mustn't get ahead of myself; I've got to pass the entrance exam first. What about you? Will you be playing cricket and football (if you get in too, but I'm sure you will)?

A girl has just been expelled from school for smoking. You might think that a lot of people smoke (not me), but she wasn't just smoking - she was smoking drugs! None of us know anything about drugs. Where did she get them? What's it like? What's it even called? We think it must be marijuana, which apparently comes from Mexico or somewhere. It's all very exciting, anyway, and all the parents are deeply shocked of course. Most of them think she must be very fast, but I'm not sure what drugs have got to do with being fast. Anyway, I will keep you informed.

It was good to hear your news about what you're reading and what your housemaster is like and what James Pringle thinks about the monarchy and how Norwich City are doing. No-one else here gets letters like that and they are all very jealous! (No, I don't read them out, in case you're worried, but I give them little titbits to get them going.) Please write again soon. Tell me what you think about the Cuban crisis! (Do you think about the Cuban crisis? Do you think we nearly had a nuclear war until they backed down?) Or tell me about football, then I will tell you about hockey.

Yours sincerely,

Hettie

TWENTY-THREE

"What are you going to do at Oxford, Hutton?"

"I've got to get there first. A-levels, S-levels, entrance exam. I might be too thick."

"Tell them your father was a war hero. Or better still, tell them he went to Oxford. I don't suppose he endowed a scholarship anywhere?"

They laughed. "No, he didn't. And everyone's father was a war hero. All my father did was get killed, I'm afraid."

"That should be good enough. I wish my father had been killed. It'd help no end."

"Pringle, that's disgusting. And what'd help a lot more would be if you did a bit of work. That's how you get into university. Anyway, what are you going to do?"

"Well, first of all I'm not going to Oxford. I'm going to either Cambridge or London."

"London? What for?"

"Politics. You can do politics at LSE. And London's where it happens, isn't it?"

"I don't know. I suppose so. Where what happens?"

"It. Life. Love. Power. Sex."

"Oh, sex. I think that happens in lots of places. So I've heard."

"Not as much as in London. People are much more loose. I have it on good authority."

"How good? Whose authority?"

"I read about it in Men Only." They both laughed again.

"Well, I think you ought to start working, Pringle. Wherever you go, you've got to get your A-levels."

"On the other hand, I might just work on a building site. It pays a lot better."

"You could, I suppose. Is there plenty of sex?"

"Not on the site, I don't think. But the money helps you buy drinks. And you know what drinks mean."

"Perhaps we should all go and work on building sites. Best of all, maybe we should work on building sites in Oxford. Build in the day, arrange our tutorials for five o'clock, study in the evenings."

"Except we'd be having sex in the evenings."

"Oh, I forgot that. Maybe study at weekends. And there's got to be time for cricket, too."

Pringle was sipping a gin and tonic. Nicholas had declined the offer of one. It was Sunday night, a grim and depressing time at school. Neither of them had had an exeat that weekend. Nicholas had played a football match for the school the day before, but the match had been drawn and he had not played well. On Sunday morning after chapel he had written to Helena. On Sunday afternoon he had been bored. Now they had nothing to look forward to except Monday. At home, neither of them was ever bored. Nicholas went round the farm or read a book in the warmth of the kitchen. Pringle spent most of his time wandering round town or hating his father, both of which he enjoyed indolently. Neither of them wanted to be at school.

But there they were, and they were stuck.

"What do you want to do when you leave university, Pringle?"

"Christ, I don't know. Do you?"

"Think about it."

"What do you mean?"

"I want to spend a few years thinking about it. There's no need to hurry. We can always get jobs. I thought about working on the farm."

"For good? For life?"

"Well, maybe. It's great there. But I'm no good at the mechanical bits. I don't think I drive a tractor very well. And it's bloody cold in winter. Maybe I'll just work on it in summer when they need me."

"And in winter?"

"I thought I might go to London. Get a job somewhere. Work in a bar. I don't know. Will they let you just work in winter? Save up and take the summer off?"

"Sounds a good idea to me. The whole world ought to do it. I suppose someone has to work in summer, though, otherwise the trains and buses and things wouldn't take us to the places to be idle in. And the shops to sell us food while we're idle."

"It doesn't mean that you and I have to work in summer though. We're too young."

"You're getting to sound political, Hutton. Or something like that. We're the young people."

"What about you then, Pringle? What are you going to do?"

"Well, first of all I'm going to Greece. Afghanistan. India. In the summer vacs."

"Vacs? What's a vac? Is it like a van?"

"You've got to pick up the lingo, Hutton. It's the vacation. From the university. The long vac is after the summer term. It's the summer holidays. It lasts from the middle of June until October. You can work for two months then go abroad for two months. Want to come?"

"You mean, miss harvest?"

"Whenever harvest is, yes, you might miss it. When is it?"

"End of July to September."

"Yeah, you could miss some of it."

"No. That's not possible. I couldn't let them down. And I'm not sure I want to go abroad, anyhow. I'm happy here. What do you want to go abroad for?"

"Adventure. See the world. Culture. Sex. All that."

"There's only one of them I really want. And I might get that at home, you never know." He thought of Millie, his unrepeated experience with her. Would it ever happen again, with her or anyone else? Would it be more likely to happen abroad?

They went back to their books. Nicholas scanned his history prep. It was an unavoidable fact of nature that he was bored rigid with history. History went inevitably with English at A-level; it was assumed that the same people wanted to do both, though he never knew why. Nicholas could pass history if they insisted. What he wanted, though, was to read books.

Of course there was more to life than reading books, so he listed the other things he wanted to do. Cricket. Football. Talk to girls. In reverse order.

Well, sleep with girls actually, but that was over the horizon. Talking would have to suffice.

He never asked himself what he would do, or whether there was more chance of fulfilling his desires, if he did not go to university. His mother expected him to go. His school expected him to go. His contemporaries expected him to go. What was more, they all expected him to go to Oxford. If he failed, he would try redbrick universities. To be honest, though, he did not expect to fail. Why should he?

Twenty-Four

Nicholas stood in two inches of water swirling round his boots. He had given up trying to push it away. The machine just leaked and nothing could be done about it. The noise pounded relentlessly. He took a full sack from the spout, swung it over the wet floor and dumped it with the others on the pallet waiting to be tied. "Take the fucking pallet," Khan said, so he did. The trolley fitted underneath the pallet and he wheeled it into the gantry. Someone else would take it from there.

"Fucking all right, Nicky?" Khan asked.

"Fucking all right, Khan. You all right?"

"All right." Neither of them could hear the other but they could guess what each was saying. Another sack filled and this time it was Khan's turn. They were tired. It was near the end of the shift. Then it would be overtime.

Neither of them knew what was inside the sacks. When he started, Nicholas asked someone what the powder was. "Brown powder," he was told. Another one was white powder. It might have been starch, it might have been flour, it might have been neither. All they knew was that the sack filled, they took it off the machine, they put it on a pallet and it got loaded up. It didn't matter what was in it.

"Fucking near time," Khan shouted at him.

"Yeah."

"You on overtime?"

"Yeah."

"Humping?"

"Yeah."

"Fucking right."

"You too?"

"Fucking joking."

This could mean either yes or no. It didn't matter which. Either Khan would be there or he wouldn't. Probably he would. He worked overtime every day except during Ramadan, when he did not have the strength. On pay day he went to the post office and sent a ten pound note back home. He was building a house there.

The machine broke down. It was half an hour from the end of the shift. Khan and Nicholas grinned at each other and made their way to the boiling water tap. While the maintenance man was summoned they sat on the sacks and drank tea. Nicholas fell instantly asleep. The machine would take nearly an hour to fix and he was finished with it for the day.

It was two o'clock in the afternoon, the end of the morning shift. In Britain this was known as the continental shift system. On the continent it was known as the English system. Morning shift from six till two, graveyard shift from two till ten and night shift from ten till six. Three shifts of eight hours each, alternating. Overtime was four hours. On the morning shift you worked overtime in the afternoon, on the graveyard shift you worked it in the morning and on the night shift you came in at six. It was hard to tell who was on what shift because you were all there all the time.

Nicholas had been catching a train to Oxford. He was going to visit his friend Madeleine, who was still there because she was doing an MA. However, the train broke down just after Slough and the passengers were obliged to climb down and walk back beside the track to the station. As it happened, Nicholas only had a ticket as far as Ealing Broadway so he took the opportunity to bypass the station and walk towards the town.

The Employment Exchange was situated in the trading estate and suggested in its window that Slough was a fine place to work, that there was overtime available in every job advertised within and that milk, honey and inestimable wealth were the reward of those who enquired within. Slough was not as keen to welcome Nicholas, however, as he had been led to believe. At the desk, a tired man with a beard told him he could be a milkman or a postman or work at Mars if he didn't have eczema or dermatitis. The only other alternative was Modern Products, the factory beside the railway line that was covered in white powder. The bearded man made a telephone call and half an hour later Nicholas was at the gate.

Mr Lewis was the man to talk to. He was found in a large, sweaty building diagonally across from the main gate. He wore a tie but was struggling out of an overall when Nicholas handed him his interview card.

"You're the one they rang about."

"I came after a job."

"Didn't think you'd come to sweep the chimney. Been working?"

"I had a job in the summer. Before that I was, well, a student."

"Student. Jesus. Speak Hindi, by any chance?"

"No, I'm afraid not."

"Pity. Still, student, you'll probably pick it up. You fit?"

"Not too bad. I play cricket. And football."

Mr Lewis made a strange sound, somewhere between a choke and a guffaw. He looked at the interview card. Then he stared for a short while out of the window, apparently reflecting on the futility of life. Finally he remembered that he was conducting a job interview.

"Start on Monday," he said. "Six o'clock, that's in the morning, when the sun rises. Bring your cards. Clocking on bonus if you're here by quarter to. Basic twenty quid a week, plenty of overtime, clothes allowance after three months. Ask for Arthur, he's morning foreman next week. Oh, and you work a week in hand."

Nicholas had no idea what this meant. He also had no idea whether he wanted to take the job. However, twenty quid a week seemed like a lot of money and he could save hard through the winter. If he could find a bedsit and an alarm clock he could stick it out at least until Christmas. Next year would take care of itself.

The alarm clock worked better than it was asked to, waking him at four o'clock instead of five. His bedsit, advertised at £20 per calendar month, was cold. He made tea, ate some spaghetti left over from the night before and walked to Modern Products. He arrived at 5.35 and found Arthur in a glass booth on the edge of the main building.

"Fuck me," Arthur greeted him. "You out of nappies?"

"Last week," Nicholas told him. He didn't need the job that badly.

"Know the difference between an Indian and a Pakistani?"

"To look at?"

"Unless you want to smell them. Me neither. They'll tell you. They're all right if you let 'em alone. We were going to put you on a machine with the whites but we need someone on sacking off. They'll tell you what to do."

"Thank you."

"Don't thank me, thank the firm, it's them exploiting you. See if you last the week."

Outside the glass booth, noise hammered at the skull like an artillery barrage. Water, sawdust and powder mixed all over the floor. Sacks, cloth and paper bags lay in piles, some full, some empty and some burst. Small machines whirred and grunted, large machines thumped and pounded; liquid and powder oozed out. Men stood watching the machines, occasionally turning a dial.

In the distance a row of large vats held liquid that entered or left the machines. Occasionally a man climbed a ladder and looked in them. Other men walked from one machine to another, their purpose unclear. Everyone was filthy, covered in white powder and dark dirt, the two melded together with water. In one corner two Asians and a black man stood in front of a sacking off machine. Arthur went over to them.

"This here's Khan," he said.

"Morning, Khan."

"What you say your name was?"

"Nicholas."

"Khan, show Nick the ropes."

"Where's your boots?" Khan asked.

"I didn't know I needed boots."

The other men looked at each other. The black man sucked his teeth.

"Fuckin' what?" he said to Khan.

"Fuckin' what," Khan said.

"I need boots?"

Over most of the factory the water lay as a damp covering, sticking the boots to the floor. In front of the sacking off machine, however, it was an inch deep. All the men brought in water boots and left them beside the machine.

"Watch me," Khan said. No more was mentioned of the boots. Khan waited in front of the machine until a sack became full, then detached it, lowered it on to the scales and weighed it. He took out a little powder and tipped it in a bin, weighed the sack again and tied it with string. He swung it across to the waiting pallet.

"Next fucking sack yours," he said. "168 pounds. I help you."

One and a half hundredweight. Nicholas had carried two hundredweight sacks of barley - two stone or one coomb - on the farm at home. It shouldn't be impossible. The sack filled. Khan told him when to make his move. He lowered the sack, forgot to release the clippers that held it and filled the sack too full. They baled out powder together. Nicholas muttered his thanks but got no response. He weighed the sack until it was right, then tied it and lifted it across to the pallet. He had taken so long that the next sack, which someone had fixed to the spout, was already full and needing to be removed.

"Take it turns," Khan said. "Easy fucking peasy. Hard work."

There was no doubt about that. By the time two o'clock came round, Nicholas could scarcely walk to the gate. His feet were frozen. No overtime was offered on the first week. They wanted to see if you turned up next morning before they offered overtime.

He bought a pair of water boots, went home, ate some more spaghetti and went to bed.

Hettie was working for the BBC. On leaving Oxford, she had done a secretarial course because women had to. Men were accepted on to BBC traineeships, women did secretarial courses. Then a first class degree in English or Modern Languages became an asset again and she found a job at the BBC and a flat with two other secretaries in Hammersmith.

JEREMY CAMERON

"So you take dictation?" Nicholas asked. "You make the tea? You buy their wives' Christmas presents for them?"

"Don't forget sleeping with them."

"You sleep with them?"

"No, I don't, actually. If only because they haven't asked me. But I do the rest."

"Hettie, you must be ten times cleverer than those bastards. All they do is make TV programmes, there's nothing smart about that."

"Well, there is, actually. When I'm a programme maker I hope you'll tell me I'm smart. But I have to do this first. They don't take women without a secretarial course."

"Is that official?"

"No, of course it's not official. But it's reality. Have some more wine."

They sat in Hettie's bedroom drinking cheap wine and smoking a joint and he looked at her legs. They stretched up endlessly, bare, covered only briefly by a pale green mini-skirt. She leaned over towards him and he looked down her top while she poured him some more wine. It puzzled him now, as it had puzzled him for three years, that Hettie had never slept with him. Actually he had never asked her but that was due to fear of rejection. She was lovely and clever and athletic. They must be queuing up at the BBC.

"Do you remember that night you got very drunk at Pringle's party at his flat on the Iffley Rd?" After all his protestations, Pringle had gone to Oxford too.

"Well, I don't remember much about it, Nicholas, but you've mentioned it on the odd occasion. Twice a week, approximately, for the last three years."

"And I put you to bed in his spare room?"

"Yes, I know."

"I never told you that I took a bit of a look at your breasts though, did I?"

She laughed. "You dirty beast! Nicholas, our relationship is supposed to be a meeting of minds! Did you enjoy it? Were they nice?"

"You weren't wearing a bra, you see, so I had to have a look. They were very nice, actually."

"And my vagina? Did you have a look at that too? Was that nice?"

"I don't know. I didn't look. I wish I had."

They both laughed.

"Why didn't we ever do it together, Hettie? I know you had lots of other boyfriends but you could have found time for me."

"You were my friend, Nicholas. I want you to be always my friend. When we're eighty five I want to be talking about books with you and getting drunk with you. I don't want the other thing to get in the way."

"Your husband might not like us getting drunk together when we're eighty five."

"He can like what he wants. What are you reading at the moment? Anyway, you were busy with other girls, as far as I can remember. What about that what's-her-name, Madeleine, that clever girl from St Hugh's, you spent a lot of time with her."

"It took me nearly a year to get her into bed."

"A year! Bloody hell, Nicholas, I never lasted longer than a week. When the wind was right."

They laughed again.

"Anyway, you can sleep with me tonight if you like. It's warmer than the floor. But no sex. Or, at least, not unless I really insist. Now tell me about this job of yours. And what you're reading."

"I'm reading Dashiell Hammett. The Thin Man."

"I'm reading Margaret Drabble. Jerusalem The Golden."

"Graham Greene. The Comedians."

"I read that too. And Alan Paton. Cry, The Beloved Country. Fabulous."

"Jean Rhys? The Wide Sargasso Sea?"

"I haven't read that yet. Is it good?"

"Far out. Elizabeth Taylor. Angel."

"Françoise Sagan. La Chamade."

"Kingsley Amis. Take A Girl Like You."

"He's becoming a bit reactionary. Let me put some music on. Stones or Dylan?"

"Sergeant Pepper?"

"Again? We played it all summer after we'd finished our finals, didn't we? I think we played it for three weeks solid."

""I read the news today, oh boy...""

""About a lucky man who made the grade...""

""And though the news was rather sad...""

""Well, I just had to laugh... I saw the photograph...""

""He blew his mind out in a car...""

""He didn't notice that the lights had changed...""

""And all the people stood and stared...""

""They'd seen his face before...""

In unison: ""Nobody was really sure if he was from the House of Lords...""

They laughed together and smoked their joint and drank beer and sang the rest of the song. A Day In The Life, the epitome of the Beatles, a song of sunshine and showers, had dominated their year and perhaps the whole of their future lives. They realised that already, at twenty three, they were nostalgic for a supposed golden past.

"I read The Groucho Letters. They weren't very good. I was expecting a barrel of laughs."

"Do you remember when we went to see A Night At the Opera at Headington? There was so much laughing we had to go back the next afternoon to hear the words."

"There was nearly as much laughing then. But that was us."

"I read Saul Bellow. Seize The Day. Bloody boring. Don't read it."

"I won't. I've read all the John le Carré now."

"That's because you knew his brother Rupert in Magdalen. But he's good. I didn't bother with the detective stories though. Have you read V.S. Naipaul? The Mimic Men? You've got to."

"I will."

They played The Byrds and Julie Driscoll and Manfred Mann ("If you gotta go, go now, or else you gotta stay all night" had caused many a stir in college television rooms) and the Kinks and the Stones and Donovan and, of course, Dylan. Then they played Sergeant Pepper again.

It was two o'clock. Hettie had only a single bed in her bedroom. When Nicholas crept in beside her she was already asleep.

He lay there and thought about sex at university. So close to her body - in fact touching her body - there was little else he could think about. He had been convinced at university that everyone else was having sex and he was the odd one out. It was nearly three years before he discovered that everyone else thought the same thing. Then Madeleine slept with him, the night before finals started of all times, and he thought that perhaps he had arrived after all. Then he found out that everyone else had done the same thing. Except that they had waited until finals had ended.

Oxford had been a failure, sex-wise. There weren't enough girls to go round, even if they went round fast, and they all seemed to be taken by confident Old Wykehamists who didn't even have to try very hard. Old Etonians never got girls at Oxford because they were generally thought too stupid, but Wykehamists were thought to be bright as well as debonair. The Etonians imported girls from home who were as stupid as they were, or pretended to be. As for the rest, the grammar school boys and the minor public school types, they had to hope for the best. There were girls at parties, there were girls at lectures and in libraries and on tennis courts, there were girls at secretarial colleges in the city and there were girls in geographical societies. It was tough getting near any of them, though.

Then Madeleine came along. She was short and dark and astoundingly clever, a combination which fortunately put most men off. She did Chinese and played lacrosse for the university. Nicholas met her at a meeting of a student magazine and was immediately attracted when she said she wanted to write about women's sport. She was ignored at the meeting. No-one wrote about sport. Especially not women's sport.

They went for a drink together and next day he watched her play lacrosse. He was amazed at how violent she was. On the basis of her cleverness and her outrageous physicality he thought she might sleep with him. He was wrong.

For a year they talked about sport and student magazines and Chinese languages, which he pretended to be interested in so that she might sleep with him. They were both working for their finals and both playing sports so they met only on Saturdays when they went to the cinema and got drunk. They even visited each other's homes in the vacations; Madeleine liked Helena and the feeling was mutual, and Nicholas quite liked her earnest intellectual parents who talked about the Abyssinian war and Wittgenstein. Still she would not sleep with him. They never fell out about it. They kissed, they felt each other up but she kept her final garments on, then they went back to talking. Until the night before finals: then she said it was about time they had sex. She said it was like going to war. You had to do it now in case you never came back.

So they did.

After finals, they did it again.

Madeleine was, inevitably, going to carry on in the next academic year and do an MA. Nicholas went back to see her at Oxford once or twice, then it petered out. She said she might sleep with her professor.

He reflected on all this while he lay beside Hettie. He thought Hettie might have a change of heart too if he woke her up by stroking her breasts. They were, after all, within a millimetre of his hands.

He never knew whether she would have done or not because she turned over in her sleep and then her breasts were on the other side of her. Well, they were on the same side of her but the other side from him.

TWENTY-FIVE

Overtime generally meant working on the humping gang. All the permanent humping gang were West Indian. It was never clear why they were all West Indian. Perhaps no one else would tolerate it. They took sacks from the pallets, placed them on an elevator and stacked them in the warehouse or straight on to a lorry. They moved slowly and seldom spoke; it was a long day to get through. They worked twelve hours straight through, humping sacks.

The first time Nicholas went on overtime, he climbed up to the upper floor and took sacks from the elevator as fast as they could be loaded up. The rest of the gang stared. Some cursed, others laughed. Within half an hour he was walking like a West Indian, shuffling slowly, pacing himself through the heat of the day. This was bloody hard work. Allowing for the noise and the dust combined with the heat, it was an inferno. Even keeping his balance on the sacks or uneven floors was nearly impossible. At the end of four hours overtime he was a broken man.

For the first month of overtime no-one spoke to him except to tell him to take the fucking pallet or start the fucking motor. He worked, went home, slept, saw Hettie at weekends. He saved a lot of money. There was nowhere to spend it and no time to spend it in. And his own job on the machine, before the overtime, came to seem easy.

It was near the end of a morning shift when a sack broke on the machine. It had been overloaded - the Indian working on it, Ali, had inadvertently knocked the level and filled it twice. The machine protested and jammed. Powder flooded into the water on the floor, creating a mushy paste. Everyone congratulated Ali and went for a breather. Khan and Nicholas found their cups and went over to the hot water tap.

The foreman, Arthur, came over, cursed and sent for the maintenance mechanic. The mechanic had been busy on one of the big tanks and was grimy and flushed. He took a look at the machine, whirled furiously towards the workforce and demanded "Who did this lot, eh?"

"Me, Frank. It was me." Ali raised his hand.

"You fucking clumsy Asian paddy. The fuck I told you don't ever touch that fucking switch, eh?" Frank was growing red all the way down his neck.

"Sorry, Frank. It was an accident. I just knocked it."

"Sorry! Sorry! You just held up the whole fuckin' factory! And stopped me going home! Sorry! You fuckin' thick fuckin' stupid Asian bastard! Why don't you go back where you fuckin' belong, you arsehole?"

"Hey, Frank," Nicholas said. No-one else spoke.

Suddenly Frank started shoving Ali against the sacks. Then he hit him hard in the stomach. Everyone looked round for Arthur but he was nowhere to be seen. "Bleedin' fuckin' coon paddy fuckin' idiot!" Frank shouted. He hit Ali again. Ali did not retaliate. Frank appeared to have lost control altogether. No-one stepped in. The Asians stared open-mouthed. The West Indians walked away, taking off their overalls before going home. Frank grabbed Ali by the shoulders and threw him on to the sacks. Then he started looking round for a weapon, a hammer or a pole or a wooden club.

"That's enough, Frank," Nicholas said.

Frank took no notice.

"I said that's enough!" The Asians stood up. The West Indians came back to watch.

Arthur appeared. "All right, men, back to work," he told them loudly.

Then Frank turned to Nicholas. Now he was completely out of control, his eyes bulging, his fists clenching and unclenching. In his hand was a spanner.

"You fuckin' Paki-loving scum!" he yelled at Nicholas. "Fuck off back to Moscow and take all your fuckin' Asian shitheads back with you, you fuckin' bastard cunt!"

There was no point in waiting to see what Frank would do with the spanner. Nicholas walked up to him, hit him very hard in the solar plexus, turned him round, grabbed him by the shoulders and threw him to the ground. Then he brought his heel down on his stomach, took the spanner from his hand and sat on him. Frank was retching helplessly, gasping for air.

Phew, Nicholas thought. Did I do that? Was that me?

Silence, or as near silence as there could be, ruled for several seconds over the factory.

Then the West Indians whistled and applauded.

The Asians stayed quiet.

"All right," Arthur announced. "You, get off him. All you others, go home, end of shift, you'll be paid up till normal time. See you tomorrow."

Nicholas rose. Frank still lay there. Everyone slowly dispersed, like a wave trickling back haphazardly from the beach. No-one said anything. They took their clothes, their mugs and their lunch packs, clocked off and made their way to the factory gate.

As they all turned to go their separate ways, an Indian called Ravi came up to Nicholas.

"I go to see union man," he said. "There will be plenty trouble. I go with my friend Ali you helped. We tell union man what happened."

"What about management?"

"Fuck management. I go to see union man. Everything all right. You see."

The night shift finished at six in the morning. Nicholas had been on overtime from six the previous evening so he had done twelve hours. He walked home in the dark, looking forward to a few hours' sleep before going back at six for more overtime. He wondered whether it was a bonus to be asleep when everyone else was awake, or a curse.

It was a surprise to find a trail of powder running ahead of him, clearly leaked from a sack, probably of flour. I must be hallucinating, he thought, without benefit of drugs; I'm seeing things at home that I've been seeing all night. It's got to me, I'm now officially barmy.

Fifty yards from his front door, a young woman was sitting on the pavement under a sack.

No, he thought, I am not hallucinating. There are no young women at work. Nor old women. This is happening here.

"Can you please get this bloody thing off me?" she asked him.

One thing Nicholas could do was lift a sack of flour. "Be glad to," he said. He picked up the sack and slung it over his shoulder. Then he pointed out the line of powder that lay behind them. "Is it a trail for the hounds?" he asked.

"Shit." She had evidently not known.

"Where to?"

"58."

"That's my address." Was he really hallucinating? Then he realised she might think he had made it up and was pursuing her. "I live in Room C. I'm Nicholas."

"I'm Cindy."

"Are you the new tenant in Room F? The one who left a bottle of Biostrath elixir outside all our doors?"

"It's nectar. It's the answer to our world's problems. It makes us peaceful and healthy."

"I'm not sure the people in 58 want to be either of those. Where have you come from with this bag of flour?"

"Scotland."

"On the train?"

"I hitched."

"Overnight? With a sack of flour?"

"Yes. Thank you for carrying my sack. This is our house."

"Why didn't you buy a sack down here?"

"My folks ground the flour. Can you bring it to my room?"

They entered the building and walked upstairs. Without checking, Nicholas knew that it was a one hundredweight sack of flour, minus the trail left behind. Even with his experience, it was no joke carrying it up the stairs. He was sweating when he reached her door.

"Thank you so much. I'm really grateful. I need to go to sleep now. And have a bath."

"Me too. I've been working all night."

"What do you do?"

"I lift sacks."

"Ah."

"And you?"

"I'm learning to be a teacher. I'm going to teach botany and cookery."

"Healthy cookery?"

"Yes." They entered her room and he laid the sack on the floor. It had trailed flour all the way up the stairs. "Would you like to eat something healthy later?"

"I have to leave for work at 5.15."

"Four o'clock."

"Thank you very much." He had a feeling he would not like her food. But she had bright green eyes. And long blonde hair.

He went straight to bed and slept until three. He made a cup of tea and a piece of toast, then soaked in the bath, his tea resting on the stool beside him. The bathroom was shared and he realised he might be keeping the new tenant from her ablutions, so he climbed out, shaved, dried and dressed and went back to his room. Normally this would have been the extent of his social life before going back to work. This time, having heard no sign of life from Room F, he went up at four o'clock and knocked cautiously on her door.

It opened instantly. Cindy was freshly washed, brushed and combed and wearing a different granny dress. "Hi!" she announced. "You're awake!"

"So are you. But you're very quiet. And you've put flowers in." Over the course of the day the room had been transformed. Flowers and plants of all colours and sizes stood on tables and ledges and chairs. He realised there was no bed. Incense burned. Music was playing very softly; The Incredible String Band were weaving their mysterious tendrils of sound. "You're a hippy then," he added. "A flower child. My mother warned me against you."

"What did she say? Be careful of all that music and flowers and love?"

"Along those lines. I think it may have been the drugs. Your room looks very nice. I've never been in it before." The tenants of the house only passed the time of day if they met on the stairs, which was seldom.

"The man who was in here died, did you know that?"

"Died? My God."

"That's quite a trip, am I right?"

"Far out. I thought I hadn't seen him lately. He probably didn't take enough Biostrath."

"Camomile or Dandelion?" she asked, motioning him to a seat. He thought it was a choice of first course until he saw the kettle boiling on the hot plate.

"Yes, please."

She placed a hot drink and then a plate of food before him. The light was dim and he was not sure what he was eating. It was not meat or fish and it was raw. There was brown rice which was cooked. There was something mushy and there were some green leaves. None of it came from any shop he knew but it was better than spaghetti again.

For half an hour they made polite conversation. She told him about her teacher training course and he told her about Modern Products. He made it sound quite attractive. They compared families. She had two parents, one more than him, and a brother, also one more than him. He told her about Terry, who was almost a brother, and Bill, who was almost a father.

"What time did you have to leave, did you say?"

"Quarter past five. Clocking on bonus is at quarter to six."

"You don't want to miss that."

"I don't."

They looked at each other. It was quarter to five.

They stood up together and moved so that they were touching.

Cindy took off her dress. She had nothing underneath except a pair of panties. She was slim and small breasted and very exciting.

"You have to take something off too," she said. "In fact you have to take a lot of things off."

I didn't think this would happen to me in Slough, Nicholas thought. In fact I didn't think it would happen to me anywhere any more. He took off all his clothes, every one of them.

"That's not fair," she said. "You're ahead of me." She took off her panties.

"Where do we lie down? Do we lie down?"

She pulled a very thin mattress from under a chest of drawers and lay on it. There was no pillow and no bedding. He lay beside her and touched her side. "Christ almighty," he said.

"My petal," she said floweringly.

"Is it safe?" he asked, as he should.

"I'm not going to tell you." Then she laughed as she saw the horror on his face. "Yes, of course it's safe, my lovely. Come here."

They laughed and rolled together, over and under, moving round, kissing and hissing, negotiating, touching and tasting all over. She held him in her hand and examined him with a quizzical look. He slid his hand between her legs as she knelt above him and she lowered her breasts to his mouth. They rolled together again, then back, and she lay on him and parted her legs and took him inside her and moved with him backwards and forwards. It was easy, it was simple and very soon he could let go because she started to shudder and gave out a little cry. He came inside her with gratitude and happiness and she lay on top of him still moving, her head on his neck. Then they were still.

"Oh my," she said.

"Cindy, Cindy, Cindy... "

"I hope you aren't late for work."

"I'll run."

"You'll miss your clocking on bonus."

"Bugger the clocking on bonus. You're worth it."

"I'm flattered."

They laughed and he came out of her and she groaned her disappointment. Then she got up and found some tissues and they mopped themselves up. They giggled.

"That was fantastic," he said. "Fab. Cindy, that was just lovely."

"It was."

They laughed once more. He wondered whether they would do it again some time. Then she waved him off and he went to his room to change into work clothes, still dirty from the night before. He hurried off to the factory.

Twenty-Six

Ravi came over at the first break and said "Nick, you must go to see union man in dinner hour tomorrow. He is waiting for you."

"Dinner hour? I'm on nights, Ravi. I shall be asleep then."

"You can sleep next day. I explain him what happen, he is waiting for you tomorrow. I take my friend you helped to him, we explain everything. He sort it out."

"Thanks, Ravi. I'll be there."

Nicholas went home at six next day, slept until 11.30 and went to the union office. It was a tarted up shed with a kettle and a few files, where the convenor drank tea and dealt with complaints in the dinner hour. The factory had only a dozen shop stewards so convenor was a grand term; but he collected the dues and insurance and advertised union facilities. He also sorted out local problems. Then once a year the bosses pulled out some sherry before lunch and handed round cigarettes and negotiated a cost of living increase. Once every three years, a union full-timer came in and sorted out a proper pay increase, including overtime rates and a productivity deal.

Nicholas knocked and entered. He knew the convenor by sight, a working convenor called Harold Tebb from the driving pool. Another man sat at the table, the steward from the sacking section, an anonymous figure called Fergus, one of the few white men in the section.

"Mr Tebb?"

"Come in. I'm Harold Tebb. You must be young Nick. Come in and sit down, have a cup of tea." He shook hands and pulled out a chair.

"Sorry to bother you with all this," Nicholas said. "I'd have let it rest there. I don't know if management know about it. Arthur hasn't said anything."

"Best we know about it, though. The union generally sorts out these sorts of incidents. Don't want management interfering. Take sugar? I dare say you've got out of bed, have you?"

"Doesn't matter."

"Doesn't matter, good. Now, Fergus here tells me you hit the mechanic, Frank Mellor, right? Then one of the Asians came in here, Ravi somebody, told me your side of the story, understand?"

"I stopped him hitting Ali who I work with. He was going to hit him with a spanner. Or me. Yes, I hit him."

"You don't know Frank was going to hit him do you? Maybe he just wanted to frighten him. Or you."

"He called him a fucking Asian paddy and called me Paki-loving scum."

"He didn't hit you. But you hit him."

217

"Strictly, yes."

"You realise he could use the union's solicitors to take out a private summons for assault."

Nicholas laughed. He assumed it was a joke.

"Don't bloody laugh, young man. It could cost the union money. And it's a serious business, hitting one of your workmates, a maintenance man at that. Thank God it wasn't the bloody foreman, then we'd all be in the shite."

Nicholas stared. "Jesus Christ! He went for someone first, and that was a union member too!"

"Did the Indian hit him?"

"So what?"

"So it's nothing to do with you, eh? Anyhow, management don't know about it so I suppose I'll have a word with Frank and ask him to forgive and forget. And you don't bring any more of your fighting manners in here, if you please, it's been a nice quiet little factory till now."

"Me? And what about having a word with Ali and asking him to forgive and forget?"

"I already did that. And look, son, between you and me, these Asians'll keep pretty quiet if no-one stirs them up, all right? They don't give a lot of trouble and they don't go hitting Englishmen, it seems it's only other Englishmen do that."

"And they do all the dirty jobs and get abused and don't complain about the shitty conditions?"

Tebb looked up abruptly. "Where'd you get all them fancy ideas, son? College education, was it? Thought you'd do a bit of slumming, did you, or are you one of them troublemakers? Chairman Mao and that crap?"

"On our machine, mate," Nicholas said, "we stand in water twelve hours a day. Did you know that, or haven't the Asians ever complained?"

"Look, son, when I started here you were lucky to go out for a pint on a Saturday night. Now there's people driving away in new cars they've made out of this factory. And most of it's negotiated by me and others. Nobody complains about that."

"Come off it, Harold. It's the lowest wages in town, that's why only the blacks and Asians take it, and they work twelve hours a day, five days a week, more if they can get it. When did they ever see their kids at night? And when did they get their work temperature regulated or the fire escape checked or their holidays put up to three weeks a year? What were the firm's profits last year?"

"You fucking young twerp, you come in here and benefit from this union's work, like all the wogs on your section, then you shout about all we done here..."

"Work nuts. This union needs some bloody militancy in its next productivity deal." Nicholas drained his tea, turned and left the office. There obviously wasn't going to be any comeback, good or bad, from the fracas with the mechanic.

TWENTY-SEVEN

The factory normally closed down between Friday night and Monday morning but occasionally overtime came up on a Saturday. Volunteers were required. No-one wanted to work on a Saturday. Nicholas joined the humping gang at eight. Khan was there, of course. If there had been an extra day between Sunday and Monday he would have worked that too. The West Indians were subdued and grim.

They finished at twelve and clocked off at the gate. One of the West Indians, not looking up from his timecard, spoke brusquely to Nicholas.

"Saturdays after work we go down the club," he said.

"Which club?"

"You is invited." He led the way to his car, where two others were already waiting. Nicholas climbed in the back seat. The driver was George. The others were Philo and Lemoine.

The West Indian Sports and Social Club was a low, pre-fabricated building covered in wire netting, fixed broken glass and other burglar deterrents, though no sign of trouble ever materialised. George parked, led the way in and ordered four pints of Guinness. Nicholas was not asked his preference.

They sat at a table. There were no white people in the club besides him.

"You play cricket?" George asked.

"Yes. I play in Norfolk in the summer. But it's winter now." He did not add that for the last three years he had played for his college at Oxford University. The information seemed superfluous.

"We need a wicket keeper. We like to field a white wicketkeeper. To keep up appearances, you understand."

"I... are you asking me?"

It occurred to Nicholas that he had passed some test. No-one had said anything to him after the business with Ali. Nor did the West Indians talk much to the Asians. But he had not been asked to play cricket before.

"Take another pint."

He had hardly started on the first. Furthermore, drinking Guinness at lunchtime seemed a foolhardy course of action. One of the others placed a second pint in front of him.

"Thank you for the offer, George. I appreciate it."

"No training required."

"No training required!"

"No training required!" George's pronouncement brought repetitive hilarity around the room. It was not clear why no training was required for the cricket team but suddenly everyone was laughing. None of the West Indians had ever been seen to laugh at work. Nicholas laughed with them.

Then the dominoes appeared.

Dominoes in the pub at home was a quiet, seemly occupation, the players silently assessing their fives and threes and sliding them stealthily into play. Dominoes in the West Indian Sports and Social Club was not like that. It was an ear-splitting, raucous, explosive experience. Players raised a domino high and slammed it down, shouting, arguing and apparently on the brink of open warfare. The same workers who were silent, strong and taciturn at the factory had transmuted instantaneously into joking, uninhibited, volatile extroverts, given half an hour of freedom and a couple of pints of Guinness. None of them had ever treated Nicholas well at work. He was not entirely sure whether their offer of cricket stemmed from comradeship or whether the comradeship stemmed from the need for a white wicketkeeper. Things had changed, though.

"Let me buy you a drink, George," he said after the first domino hand had ended. "What'll it be?"

"This is a West Indian club," George told him. "No offence, but only black men buys drinks in here. You is white. Therefore you cannot buy drinks."

"Is the cricket team from this club?"

"Yes indeed. The West Indian Sports and Social Club first team cricket."

"Is there a second team?"

"No sir. But don't tell no-one!"

"So I can play for the cricket team even though I'm white, but I can't buy a drink."

"Yes indeed."

"That's not fair."

George put down his glass, wiped his mouth and looked Nicholas up and down. The conversations around them paused. Everyone hung on George's next words.

"Let me give you some advice, young man," he pronounced. He looked down, then up, then continued.

"In life, as in art, remember this. Never be fair. Above all, never be fair to the bosses. Or to the Conservative Party. Or to the white man. They would never be fair to you."

Then he pealed with laughter and so did everyone else.

It was advice that Nicholas took to heart.

He had been home only once in three months. He arrived home on Christmas Eve at lunchtime. Helena picked him up at the station.

Whenever Helena had picked him up from school Nicholas had been insouciant. So had she. This time, however, she ran towards him, flung her arms round him, forced him to drop all his packages and hugged him until his ribs cracked.

"Mum! Go easy!"

"Sorry, darling. My, what a huge big chap you are! You look incredible. Look at all the people staring at you. They think you're a huge big hunk of a man."

"They're staring at you, Mum. Because you're on the telly. Or because you're behaving like a lunatic." But he had nearly cried. "Now I'll have to pick all these parcels up again. Let's hope you haven't broken anything."

They packed the parcels into the car and set off. Helena nearly crashed on the first corner.

"Mum!"

"Sorry, darling. I'm afraid I'm just a bit emotional. Christmas, seeing you, all the rest of it."

"You've been mixing with too many actors, Mum. You need to keep a stiff upper lip, you know. Remember this is Norfolk."

Then they both laughed and Helena nearly crashed into the traffic lights.

"How long are you at home for?"

"Two weeks. We start work again in the new year."

"That's wonderful. It'll be like old times."

"You're not working at all?"

"I might go to London one day. But I'll be home next day at the latest."

"You're stopping overnight?"

"I might have to. We'll see."

As always, something was unspoken when Helena was gone for the night. Nicholas preferred it that way. He saw nothing to be gained from total honesty.

They reached home, turning from the road into the farmyard. Bill could be seen in the tractor shed, cleaning up some machinery.

Nicholas knew he would not come out; that was not his way. He went over.

"Bill?"

"There you are then. Where've you been?"

"Couldn't get home any sooner."

"Look at the sight of you. Bloody wars, bigger than I am."

"Need help getting the cows in?"

"Dare say you can make yourself useful. Ernie buggered off to do his shopping. Buy his wife a mink coat, I reckon, all the money I give him."

"I'll just have a bit of dinner then, take these things in, if that's all right."

"Don't leave it too late or I'll send the cows in after you. Dark at three."

"I'll be there."

Little more was said. Later, as they sat milking, Bill told him he was thinking of getting out of cattle. There was no money in it and he was getting older; and they needed feeding and milking. Stick to corn and sugar beet, they didn't want to see you every day and they didn't fight back. Bill said the beet harvest was going well. And he had got a good price for some barley he had held back at harvest.

Then he said it been cold lately, too cold, but not like the winter of '62-'63. Then he asked him when he was getting married.

"Married! Bloody hell, Bill, I'm not getting married!"

"Not never?"

"Not if I can help it. Maybe when I'm forty. I'm young, Bill, I don't want to get married."

"You courting down there?"

"No... nothing like that."

"Don't seem too sure though."

"I've been working all the time. Twelve hours a day. No time for courting."

"What's her name, this young lady?"

"There's no-one special..."

"Don't want to make Millie jealous, do we?"

"What? Who?"

"Young Millie. Not so young now. From up the hall. She was round asking for you the other day."

"Bloody hell!" he could feel the colour rising to his face, his neck, every part of him. "What did she want?"

"She never said specially what she wanted. Didn't need to."

"I can't imagine why she wanted me."

"No? That weren't what it looked like I can tell you. You wait till I tell Ernie."

"There's nothing between me and Millie. I haven't seen her for years."

Bill laughed. "Yeah, you just run on." He finished the milking. "Leaving a trail of broken hearts, I reckon. All up London too. Now, you helping me feed the cattle tomorrow, seven o'clock or what? Still manage to get up in the morning?"

"I've been getting up at five, one week in three."

"Be like a holiday for you, then."

What did Millie want? Would he want to see her? Would she want to have sex with him? Would he have qualms because of Cindy?

He didn't know the answers to the first three questions.

TWENTY-EIGHT

The greatest place in the world to be on Christmas morning was on the farm, feeding cattle. Nothing could compete: sex, cricket, food, hashish, football, music, books, nothing was as good as this. It was freezing. The frost clung to the sugar beet tops and mangolds, burning his hands through his gloves. He picked up the four tine fork instead. He stood on the trailer while Bill drove to the field, jumped down and held the gate open, then climbed back on the load. The cattle followed the trailer, munching absent-mindedly at loose tops. They drove slowly around the field, leaving a line of food on the hard, white ground. Then they broke the ice on the water trough.

Soon the cattle would have to come in for the rest of the winter; no grass was left on the field and it was getting too cold. Bill would leave them out until the last minute, though. Any food saved was money not spent.

"Just the two of you for your Christmas dinner?" Bill asked.

"No change there, Bill." But he wondered why he asked. Who had been there while he was away? "And you, Bill? Family round?"

"Lily's family. Brothers, sisters, half a dozen cousins. She's working already. Tomorrow we go round them. Here you are, here's something for your mum."

"Oh, Bill, thanks. I think she's got something for you."

"She give it to me already. Better wrapped than mine, I reckon. I never was much cop at all that. Well, I'll be getting off. Hey, looks like you've got a visitor. Bless my soul, look who it is." He started chuckling to himself, shaking quietly with mirth.

It was Millie. She was on horseback.

"Happy Christmas, Nicholas," she said from the horse.

"Thank you. Happy Christmas, Millie."

"Happy Christmas, Bill."

"Happy Christmas, Millie. Well, I think I'll be getting off." Bill made himself scarce.

"I came to give you a Christmas present. But I haven't got you anything."

"You don't have to give me anything, Millie. We haven't seen each other for six years. Where are you off to?"

"I'm going for a hack." She climbed down from her horse and tethered it. Nicholas was not too sure what hacking consisted of. "Shall we start your sherry?" she asked. "Christmas drink?"

"It's my mother's. From Bill."

She led the way into the straw shed. "Well, it'll have to be the brandy flask, then." She produced it from her jacket pocket. "Come and tell me what you've been doing, Nicholas, since I last saw you. It's ever so nice to see you again. Fancy coming across you like this."

She took a long swig from the brandy flask and passed it over. He took a shorter draught. He thought about how to describe the six years since she had seen him.

Then it became unnecessary because she sat astride him on the straw bales and started kissing him. It was disconcerting at this time of the morning - in fact it would have been disconcerting at any time - but it seemed too good an opportunity to miss. He thought only briefly of the cup of tea and piece of toast that awaited him, until she took his head and placed it under her Marks and Spencer jumper. To his astonishment he found that she was wearing nothing underneath. The jumper must have been rough against her skin. She moved her breasts around his face in what he thought was a very familiar fashion, but he thought it best not to complain.

"That's better," she said. "That's much better." She was moving up and down on him. "This is my Christmas present to you, Nicholas, I only thought of it yesterday when it was too late to go to the shops." She was licking his ear, then she rolled over and pulled him on top of her.

No more than thirty seconds later she had taken off her riding boots and jodhpurs, never an easy task, and then her panties and his trousers and underpants.

No more than thirty seconds after that she had guided him expertly inside her and he had come with a whoosh. It all happened too fast for him to know whether she had come with him. It seemed hardly relevant.

"Whew," she said briskly. "How about that?"

He was speechless.

"Now get dressed quickly before your bottom gets cold," she told him. So he did.

"I'd better get on with my hack then," she added.

"Thank you very much," he said. It was all he could think of.

"My pleasure. Happy Christmas. We should meet up in London some time."

"I live in Slough."

"Nobody lives in Slough, Nicholas. Maybe we should meet at a demo or something in London."

"Do you go on demos?"

"All the time. They're fab. Carry a banner. Shout at the pigs. Fight against the war. Meet up afterwards. It's great."

"Happy Christmas, Millie."

"Happy Christmas, Nicholas. Now I really must get on."

He went indoors for his cup of tea and piece of toast. Helena was drinking coffee.

"You look flushed, Nicholas," she told him. "I hope you're not coming down with something. Or is it just the fresh air?"

"The fresh air, I think. I'll just go and have a bath before breakfast. I'll take my tea upstairs."

"All right."

He lay in the bath reflecting on a curious Christmas. It could only get quieter from now on. There were questions to be asked, though. Were many women like Millie? And would most people prefer unloading sugar beet tops to large family gatherings? He didn't know the answer to either.

Later they exchanged presents, mostly books and records nowadays, ate a very large lunch and snoozed through the afternoon. The telephone rang a few times. In the evening they ate cheese and celery and Christmas cake and they talked. They talked of childhood and jobs and plays and films and books and family. He told her he would give up his job in the summer and come home and play cricket and work on the farm. He knew this could not go on indefinitely but he wanted to postpone change for as long as possible. She nearly told him she was growing old and might need to change her own lifestyle. However, one advantage of being an actor - at least, being an actor in work - was that one could suspend one's disbelief and indeed one's life. So she postponed telling him she was growing old. Perhaps he would realise for himself.

TWENTY-NINE

Pringle, Willie Dodger and Nicholas met in London to watch Manchester United play Arsenal. George Best scored twice and United won two nil. It was stunning. It was joyful. George played the most sensational game that any of them had ever witnessed, or would ever witness, at any sport at any time. For an afternoon he transcended football, indeed he transcended life. He performed in a world of his own, jinking, twisting and turning, ducking and jumping, rising above tackles, gliding somewhere above the earthly level. He made them all laugh. It was a privilege to be present. George changed all their lives.

They sat afterwards in a café. Pringle was still living at home though talking continually of moving out. He was trying to get a job with a socialist newspaper, one of the far left groups. Unfortunately, even if he could decide which faction to join and even if they offered him work, it would not pay him enough to live on. He was learning photography as well in order to take pictures at demonstrations. Willie was living mostly in Norfolk, refereeing football matches; apart from this it was not clear what he was doing.

"That was the greatest experience of my life," Pringle said.

"Oh, so you like football now?"

"That's not football. That's working class ballet. It's revolutionary."

"Him and John Lennon," Nicholas said. "They've changed all our lives. And Dashiell Hammett."

"Lennon's a commie bastard," Willie put in.

"Don't be ridiculous, Willie. And so what if he is? So was Hammett, incidentally."

"He's against the Vietnam War."

"Aren't we all? And where does George Best stand on Vietnam?"

"Come On Without..."

"Come On Within..."

"You've Not Seen Nothing Like United Win..."

They sang it in the rowdy café, the adaptation by the United fans of Manfred Mann's hit The Mighty Quinn. They were elated beyond normal measure. They were ecstatic. Occasionally sport, like music, could join the spectator and the participant together in joy. It was shared freedom, it was an extension beyond normal life.

"What's on for tonight?"

"We're going to see Hair again. I've got tickets."

"Far out. That Annabel Leventon..."

"This Is The Dawning Of The Age Of Aquarius..."

"The Age Of Aquarius..."

"I Met A Boy Name Frank Mills..."

"I Don't Want The Two Dollars Back... Just Him..."

They collapsed into more laughter as they sang. Hair was the record of their generation - or at least the record of some of their generation, the people they envied and feared. It was a wonderful cornucopia of non-conformity, sex, freedom and above all music. The music would last when all else died. The show would stay with them for ever, an explosion of sound and laughter and beauty and rebellion. It was the third time they had seen it in a month. It was hard to go to work afterwards.

"Then there's a party at Hettie's. We'll sleep on her floor."

"You'd like to sleep with her, wouldn't you?"

"It's not like that between us."

"Because she won't."

"Fuck off."

They laughed.

After the show they took the tube to Hammersmith and walked to Hettie's flat. They had bought bottles of wine from the off licence and peanuts from Marks and Spencer. They had different attitudes towards the girls' flat. Nicholas was used to it by now and was not intimidated. Pringle affected insouciance. Willie was manifestly ill at ease. The bathroom door held no lock and he was terrified of a woman entering while he was seated on the toilet. Then there was female underwear everywhere. Finally, the females did not take him seriously.

The party was well under way. Candles flickered, stuck into old bottles of Mateus. Incense burned in all the rooms. Open wine bottles stood everywhere under the Red Indian hand woven blankets on the walls and the posters of Woody Guthrie and Douglas Fairbanks Snr. They opened their own bottles and stood for a moment separate, not yet involved in the maelstrom of the group.

"Well, boys," Hettie said. "Make yourselves useful. Choose the music. What do we want for the night? Drug stuff? Stomping rock? West Coast?"

"Crosby, Stills and Nash?"

"Byrds?"

"Nah. Stones. Animals. Alexis Korner. Got any Geno Washington?"

"Sure. What about you, Willie? Where does your taste lie? Star Spangled Banner? Marseillaise? Horst Wessel?"

"I like Marty Robbins, actually. But I don't suppose he's quite right for dancing."

"Marty Robbins!" They howled in derision. "Excuse me while I puke. How about Engelbert Humperdinck? Des O'Connor? Frank Sinatra?" They made retching noises.

"You may mock me now, you fools. But you wait. Country Music will be king."

"We don't like kings. We're republicans."

"That just about sums you up, too. Here you are, fortunate enough to live in one of the last bastions of a monarchical system, a true sovereignty." Willie was shouting incongruously above the raucous noises of music and voices. "What do you do? You want to throw it away, the one thing that still makes Britain great."

They fell about laughing. "You're a headcase, Willie. You're off the map. I'll bet you vote Conservative before long."

Then they all paused.

"Jesus," Hettie said. "I bet you do already."

"I will not reveal how I vote," Willie said. "But I can tell you that in a politician I look for the values of Britain. A strong Commonwealth to compete with Europe. Trade union legislation. Immigration controls."

"For black people, eh? You'll let the Australians and Canadians in. The old Commonwealth."

"You know," Nicholas said, "I remember you when you were normal, Willie. In fact you were less than normal, you were scared of a football. You still ref matches. I don't think I believe all this crap. You'll probably be an anarchist next year."

"Or a Trotskyite."

"Like the rest of us."

"So what about the war, Willie? Vietnam? You're in favour?"

"Ah. I have different views from what you might think."

"Stop the commies? The domino effect? Yellow peril?"

"I agree that the communists must be stopped. But I am inclined to think that this war is misguided."

"Well, that's a bloody relief. Now shall we have some music?"

"Jumping Jack Flash..."

"It's a gas..."

"Good to see the Stones are back to the real thing."

"Yeah, none of that shit about loving us. If the Stones love us there's really no hope for the world."

THIRTY

The West Indian Sports and Social Club preferred to play their matches away. They had no permanent home ground, so for home matches they had to hire a field. Those pitches usually had a backdrop of gasometers, sewage farms and railway lines. Furthermore, home matches involved making the tea, and some of the wives were notoriously unhappy about fulfilling their wifely duty. Away matches, on the other hand, generally brought gentle trips to leafy parts of the country where they would play on a village green and women were only too happy to do what was expected of them. This included making scones.

As summer approached, Nicholas planned his departure from Modern Products; life was calling him and it did not call him to work indoors in Slough. First, however, he had to meet his obligations. As a white man, he had been asked to keep wicket for the Sports and Social Club. As a white man, he must not let the side down.

It was April and it was cold. He had brought his kit down from home, his cricket clothes and bat and pads. However, they would not keep him warm in the harsh open fields of Berkshire. He was told that they were playing today on a beautiful hill in the middle of nowhere. He put on a vest. Then two shirts and a sweater. Then another sweater. That might be enough when he was keeping wicket. While he was waiting to bat he would wear a coat.

He was just trying everything on when a knock came on the door.

Christ! It was Cindy!

They had fallen into a pattern on a Saturday lunchtime. If he was working in the morning he would come home and have a bath while Cindy made him a snack; before they ate the snack they quickly made love. If he was not working they went out together and bought food. Then he had a bath while Cindy made him a snack. Then they ate the snack first and made slow love afterwards. Theirs was an on-off relationship, not, they both maintained, heavy; but when they were in town together their Saturday lunchtimes were sacrosanct.

"Oh my! All in white! The virgin!"

"Cindy, my God, I'm sorry, I forgot... I've got to play cricket, you see. It's away. I've got to go soon."

"Which comes first, me or cricket?"

Cindy was too young to know that this was the question no woman should ever ask.

"And not before you've let me undress you, Nicholas. Why didn't you tell me you liked dressing up as a virgin? I'm finding it very exciting, darling, a virgin whore, a male virgo intactum. It's very, very sexy indeed."

"I've got to go..." Why, he thought, were women so demanding? Didn't they understand?

Within a minute, however, it would have been hard to say who was the more demanding. Cindy proved to be stunned and intoxicated to discover that, underneath his trousers, he was wearing a jockstrap. Before she removed it she did things in that area that made him exclaim with delight. Then he tore her clothes off her and began licking her from head to toe. Then he turned her over and entered her easily from behind, his hands gripping her stomach. She pushed back against him ruthlessly and cried out with him in delight and mutual pleasure.

In a moment they were spent.

"My God, Cindy."

She giggled. "You're a rude boy, Nicholas. You made me very excited. Oh, don't leave me yet."

"I've got to go, Cindy. I've got a cricket match."

"I didn't hear you worrying about your cricket match a couple of minutes ago."

"That was then. Things have moved on now. I've got to go."

He washed briefly, dried quickly and strode out of the door, saying he would see her later.

At the club they were waiting for him. He was acutely aware that he had already let down the white race by being late. They were already in the car park. Nothing was said but his apologies were, he knew, inadequate.

And he could not stop yawning.

Half the team worked at Modern Products. George he knew, and a couple of others called Everton and Roland. A large, taciturn man named Daisy slung sacks around as if they were paper darts and seldom spoke to anyone. He sat behind Nicholas in the back seat of an ancient Humber driven by a man called Ray, slim and good looking and a bit of a dandy. The last workmate was an old, frail looking man called Herbert who Nicholas assumed would be umpire or scorer.

Three surprises affected the home team when the Social Club arrived in a village in the Berkshire countryside. The first was that ten of them were black: they were entered in the league solely as the Slough Sports and Social Club, which gave nothing away. The village team covered their initial confusion with bonhomie. The second was that the Slough team appeared not to feel the cold; none of them except for the wicketkeeper wore more than a sleeveless sweater. The third, when the teams entered the field, was that Herbert was one of the opening bowlers. One way and another, Berkshire thought they might be in for an easy afternoon.

The bonhomie was replaced by some unease when the captains tossed. The Social Club won the toss and elected to field. "We bat second," George told the opposing captain. "Black men they don't bat first. We like to see the whites of their eyes."

Nicholas put on his wicketkeeping gear and the team went out to field. They did not throw the ball around, warm up or practise any callisthenics but wandered straight to their positions. Herbert fielded at first slip. "Good afternoon, wicketkeeper," he said.

"Good afternoon, Herbert. What are our chances today?"

"Today? It depend on the playing conditions. And me and Daisy and Everton."

"Why?"

"You know why he called Everton?"

"No. Isn't he called Everton?"

"No. He real name Gladstone. But we tell them he is Everton Weekes. Over here on holiday from Barbados."

"Is he Everton Weekes?"

"No. But he always tell us he bat above Everton at school. True, he bat above Everton at school. But Everton he was five years younger! Still, he always called Everton after that."

"Is he good?"

"No. He never no good. But he scare the other team good."

"And what about our bowlers?"

"You see."

They took their positions. Daisy ran down the hill and opened the bowling. He bowled five steady, innocuous balls which the batsman patted gently back to him. The sixth ball was a beamer. It might have been dangerous if it had been fast and directed at the batsman. Instead it was directed at the wicketkeeper. It looped in a slow, inoffensive parabola past the batsman's astonished head. Nicholas lost it completely against the green and brown back ground above the sightscreen and did not find it again until it hit him gently on the forehead.

"Him don't score off that ball," Daisy announced to the world. "Well stopped, wicket."

It turned out that Daisy bowled a beamer off the last ball of every over. "Him not score off that ball," he declared each time.

"Now you see real bowling," Herbert confided after the first over.

Which, indeed, they did. Herbert was sixty two and looked seventy two. He held a clerical job at Modern Products. His appearance suggested he should be in a retirement home. He measured a four pace run up and waited quietly to begin. Then he bowled his first delivery with such venom that it took off from a length and shot past the batsman's shoulder. Unfortunately Nicholas, seeing the four pace run up, had decided to stand up to the stumps. The ball hit him a vicious thwack in the neck.

So far he had not missed a ball. Or the ball had not missed him. One hundred per cent record.

"Jesus Christ," the batsman said. "I thought he was someone's granddad. Is he always like this?"

"Depends if he turns nasty," Nicholas told him. "If he turns nasty, I should run like hell."

The next ball hit the batsman hard on the toe. "Jesus Christ!" he exclaimed again.

The third ball speared into his stomach.

"I can't take much more of this," he said. "I've got a wife and kids at home. What does he want, for God's sake?"

"All depends if he turns nasty. If he thinks you're hanging around, playing a bit negative, he may go for the jugular. My advice would be play a few shots, enter into the game."

The batsman flailed away at the next ball. It hit middle stump.

The next over was a repeat of Daisy's first over. Five steady, innocuous balls were patted back down the pitch. The last ball looped past the batsman's head. This time it also looped past Nicholas. Again he failed utterly to see it and this time it did not hit him. He grabbed frantically at fresh air and the ball went for four byes.

Then, unfortunately, he yawned.

He tried to slap his jaw shut but it was too late. He was appalled. He could not stop himself. It looked as if he did not care about the four byes, as if he was just a white man amusing himself with the darkies for the afternoon, not too bothered, just a bit of fun.

It was Cindy who was to blame.

He went immediately over to George, who was fielding in the gulley. He had to explain himself.

"George, I'm so sorry," he began. "It's like this, George, you see... I'm afraid, you know, well, I... met a friend at lunchtime, a lady friend, and we, you know... I'm sorry, George... sometimes it makes you a bit sleepy."

The outcome was not what he expected. He was more appalled at George's reaction than he was by his own behaviour.

George started laughing. He clapped his hands together, looked round the whole field and called out "Hey, Mister Umpire!"

"Mister Umpire, stop the game one minute, please! Gentlemen, gentlemen, I would like to make one brief announcement here, if you please! Our wicketkeeper would like you all to know that he is very tired this afternoon because he met a lady friend at noon and they performed a matinee. A matinee, gentlemen! A round of applause, please! I understand there will be a second performance later this evening. Thank you, Mister Umpire, we will resume the game now. Thank you, gentlemen. Thank you, wicketkeeper. I know you will continue to perform to your best endeavours in these difficult circumstances."

The whole team came over and, one by one, shook his hand. After the match, which they won, they all bought him drinks. They said he needed to keep his strength up.

THIRTY-ONE

"Christ, them bales don't get any lighter. Wha'd you put in them, Bill, lead weights?" Ernie liked a little moan. He liked a big moan even more.

"Getting old, Ernie, that's your problem. Time was you'd lift them on your lingam."

This brought hilarity to the three of them and drew the work to a halt. Bill went round to the tractor and got himself a drink. Ernie sat on a pile of bales and wiped his forehead. Nicholas lay back on the trailer, completely overcome, and gazed at the blue sky.

"Tha's your fuckin' fault, young Nick," Ernie told him. "You never heard any of that language off Bill till you brought that fuckin' book in. He darsn't hardly open his gob. Now before breakfast he's coming out with all that old talk, no holding him."

Not long before, in a secondhand bookshop in Norwich, Nicholas had found a faded old copy of the Kama Sutra. It was a book he had heard of but never seen. Having opened it, he thought he had better buy it straight away. Once he had it at home, there was only one place to read it out loud: at meal times on the farm.

At first they thought he was making it up and demanded to read the passages for themselves. On doing so, Ernie borrowed the book overnight. Then a second night. Nicholas never dared ask whether it had changed anything at home but they continued to have raucous sessions at breakfast and dinner.

"Good job that Terry in't here. Never be a girl in the village left after he got a read."

They laughed again.

Terry was in his third year in the air force. In January he had to make a choice, whether to sign up for longer or whether to come home. He had joined up in January, after harvest and sugar beet harvest. For two years he had managed to fit in his leave to help out some of the time with hay carting, harvest or the sugar beet; although, as Bill said, that wouldn't get the cattle fed in February. Bill kept his job open; he would not employ anyone else until he got a decision from Terry. Nevertheless it was hard. Bill was nearly sixty. Ernie was two or three years behind. As they both pointed out, it didn't hardly get any fuckin' easier.

They had a corn dresser now so did not have to sack everything off the combine, but it was a slow job with three men including Nicholas. Bill drove the combine, Nicholas drove the corn trailer, Ernie worked the dresser. Driving the trailer was the least skilled of the three jobs but was no sinecure. The first time he did it he failed to maintain the same speed as the combine as he drove alongside, and half a load of valuable barley spilled on the ground. After that Bill stopped the combine while he shot corn into the trailer. Nicholas took it back to the barn and shot the corn into the dresser pits before returning to the field. With three men it was a long job. They worked from seven in the morning until nine at night.

When it was wet or when there was no more corn ready to cut, a gap opened up. Bill took a load of corn to the seed merchants and the other two tidied up the barn, sacking off the corn that would not go in the bins, wheeling it to the far corners and stacking it against the walls until it should be needed. When that was all done and there was still no corn to cut, they went straw carting. Harvest would not end until nearly the end of September. It was a long old job. Even straw carting was slow with only three; one man drove the tractor to the next clump of bales and then climbed down to help pitch. It was tedious too.

"Bill," Nicholas asked at breakfast as they sat back on the bales, "what would you think about having a woman on the harvest?"

"Woman?" Bill asked. "What woman?"

"My mum can drive. She's not doing anything this week. Would you like me to ask her?"

Ernie slid back off his bale. "'Scuse me," he said. "'Scuse me, I just got a coughing fit."

"Your mum, Nick?" asked Bill. "Drive that tractor?"

"Nick never driv that tractor in a straight line," Ernie said. "Ne'er mind his mum. Nice lady, though," he added hastily.

"You asked her?" Bill enquired.

"No, I never said a word. I just thought it might help. Speed things up."

"She never do it. Bugger me. Ask a woman to go pulling ragwort or wild oats or some such, not drive a tractor at harvest."

"They did it in the war."

He had an unassailable point there and they knew it. On the other hand, they had an unassailable point too. "Your mum," Ernie said. "She's a fuckin' lady, 'scusing my French. Not a woman."

"She can drive. Driving's not heavy work."

"If she can do it," Bill said, "so can Lily. She can drive."

"Well, there you are, then."

"My missis in't doing it," Ernie said. Nicholas had never heard Ernie's wife mentioned by name. "She can pull ragwort. Feed pigs. She can't drive. Hin't never had no need for it."

"Fair enough."

They worked through the morning.

At dinner time, Bill ate a sandwich and drank his drink. He thought for a while. Then he spoke.

"You want to ask your mum?" he said. "Start by driving the trailer on straw carting? Wouldn't have to reverse. Only do that if she takes the two-wheeler up the pit with a load of corn."

"You want me to ask her now?"

"Right enough."

Half an hour later, Helena was driving the tractor between the straw bales.

—ll—

Dear Frances,

I have just had the best, best, best, best, most wonderful day of my whole life.

Never mind acting. Never mind the acclaim of the audience. Never mind the TV shows. Nothing can compare.

This will be a very short letter. It is ten o'clock. We have had supper of bread, pickles and cheese. I am just about to go to bed. I am drinking a beer. Yes, a beer. Brown ale! Bill gave it to me this evening. I have got to go to bed because tomorrow I start work at seven.

At lunch time today (sorry, dinner time) Nicholas came in from the harvest field to see me. He asked if I would come and drive the tractor!

I must say you could have knocked me over with a feather duster. They were short of men and they needed someone to drive the tractor.

Well, to cut a long story short, I put on a pair of slacks, dusted off an old jacket and got out there. Me, Frances! Famous actress! (I don't think.) Fifty six years old! My first time on a tractor! With a trailer on the back with a load of straw and a man on it!

It was easy, in fact, once you got the hang of it. I just had to drive it between the heaps of straw bales and stop. Then, when they had loaded them on the trailer, drive off again. The hard part comes tomorrow or the next day when we go on a corn trailer and have to reverse. But that's just a two-wheeler so it may be easier. Two-wheelers go the opposite way from the tractor, so they say.

Four-wheelers go the same way and are very difficult. Or something like that. Anyway, we'll see what happens. Bill's wife, Lily, is going to have a go too.

I'm so tired but I feel so great. That's all for tonight.

Oh, by the way, I had a proposal of marriage the other day. Someone new. I've been going on so long with Peter that I'd nearly forgotten there were other men. Just at the moment, though, marriage seems unimportant compared with getting the harvest in!

All my love,

Helena

THIRTY-TWO

He caught the train down from King's Lynn for the demo. It was a bright autumn day, fresh and cloudless, a good day to protest against the Vietnam War. Everyone was going to be there.

He was reading a Len Deighton novel which fitted into his jacket but was disposable if he lost it. He also had a pen and notepaper in case of finding anything worth writing down. He began writing a letter to Cindy, who was in Scotland with her parents for the weekend. He had visited her in Slough in the summer but she had not been to Norfolk.

He sat opposite the only unattached young female on the train. It was always difficult trying to pick up girls. He was happiest if they made the first move. It was easy for girls, or at least those who approached him. They would not be rejected. Rejection, however, was something that males had to live with.

He bought a cup of tea and a scone. Then he wrote a poem which he thought managed to convey his dilemma.

I don't want to bother you, ma'am,
But I'm trying to find who I am.

I'm seldom a moaner

But I've lost my persona;

Has it dropped in the tea or the jam?

He turned the piece of paper round and pushed it across the table at the girl.

She smiled widely at him, apparently pleased at his attention. For a few moments she pondered his ditty. Then she picked up his pen and wrote a reply on the back. This too appeared to be a poem. Perhaps he had picked up a poetess. He had heard that they were wild.

She pushed the paper back to him and he read it carefully.

I adore your innate animality

But I fear you've a touch of duality

Your right eye's no centre

But your left's bright magenta;

Are you firmly in touch with reality?

Nicholas had always liked clever women, but there were limits. Most notably, the limits applied when they were clearly much cleverer than he was. To compose such a poem in two minutes suggested that she was out of his league. Or, perhaps, had she written it beforehand? Was it there, ready and waiting to be used whenever she was approached by limerick-writing young men on the train?

They reached Cambridge, where Willie Dodger was due to join him. Nicholas had seldom been so pleased to see Willie, who came charging into the coach, brimming with good health and energy.

They went off to another seat and he never saw the girl again. It had been a fragment of life.

"Willie!"

"Nicholas! Haven't seen you for months! Let me tell you about this game I reffed yesterday. It was a bloodbath! I sent off four players, two spectators and a linesman! The club will be charged with failing to control its supporters. The linesman awarded a corner when the centre forward kicked the ball over the goal line from half way. Then he wanted to fight the goalie. I had to have him replaced."

"You're very authoritative, Willie."

"I brook no insubordination. If all the world was the same it would be a better place."

"We know your views on the world, Willie. Have you spoken to Pringle?"

"No. I know we're meeting at Embankment station at 12.00. Who else will be there?"

"The rest of the world. But Hettie will be there. And someone called Millie might be there. I wrote her a postcard. A couple of guys from university maybe. Even my friend Terry from home. He's on leave. I told him about it. He's in the air force."

"Got short hair, then?"

"Yes."

"Might stand out a bit." Willie's hair was fashionably down on his shoulders.

"Should be a great day. I'm a bit surprised at you though, Willie. Given your views on the commies, good to see you're still against the war. Changed sides, have you?"

To his amusement, Willie looked furtively round the carriage. "Tell you later," he muttered. "Maybe." Nicholas wanted to tell him that his secret would be safe with him but careless talk cost lives.

They reached Liverpool St and took the Circle line to Embankment.

All along the river, the demonstration grew. Wedged along the Embankment, stretching endlessly east and west, the vast patchwork multitude spread and settled. Beside the bridge stood its core, solid and unmoving, a dense heavy mass of people, so close as to be touching each other. New arrivals bred fresh streams of humanity in all directions. From Waterloo on one side, from Trafalgar Square on the other, from Westminster and St Paul's and Fleet St a quarter of a million protestors descended, glad to be there, happy in their beliefs, determined in their resistance and confident that they could win.

"WILL EVERYONE PLEASE GET BEHIND THE AD HOC COMMITTEE VAN!"

"That's not much of a slogan," Pringle said. "Ho! Ho! Ho Chi Minh!"

"HO! HO! HO CHI MINH!"

"PLEASE WILL EVERYONE GET BEHIND THE AD HOC COMMITTEE VAN! THE AD HOC COMMITTEE VAN WILL LEAD THE MARCH!"

"What's an Ad Hoc committee?" Nicholas asked. "We can shout in Latin when we march on the Vatican."

"Don't be awkward, Nicholas," Hettie told him. "They're doing their best."

"PLEASE..." the loudspeaker cried feebly. "PLEASE WILL EVERYONE GET BEHIND THE VAN NOT IN FRONT! THEN WE CAN SET OFF!"

"Shall we go for a coffee till they're ready?"

"Yeah, let's. There's a cafe up Villiers St."

They detached themselves and walked up to the café. Nicholas, Pringle, Willie, Hettie, Millie and Terry. Given the company, Nicholas was relieved that Cindy was in Scotland. Millie was in a heightened state of expectancy with red cheeks and what appeared to be glistening lips. He wondered if she had taken something. Terry was quiet but amused. He was against the war but he thought this bunch was a load of student types. Hettie was there because everyone was: everyone was against the war. Pringle was there because the revolution was about to begin. Willie, though, presented a question that needed to be pursued. They sat at two tables and Nicholas found himself alone with him.

"Now you can tell me your secret," he said.

Willie was clearly bursting with his surreptitiousness but fearful of the consequences of talking. "It can't go any further," he said. "None of that lot must know. Especially Pringle."

"Especially Pringle? He'd be pleased with that, Willie. I didn't know he was so important."

"Keep your voice down! I'm not sure I should tell you at all."

Nicholas composed himself. "All right, go ahead. I'm serious. What's the secret?"

"I'm an A.P."

"What? What's an A.P.?"

"Agent Provocateur."

"You're not serious."

Willie almost visibly swelled with pride. "I was contacted. Can't tell you who by. Because my views were known but I mixed with, well, people like you and Pringle. They asked me to give a bit of help. To the country."

"To the country?"

"Patriotic. That's what it is. To deal with these outside agitators. Commie foreigners, stirring it up. We're not against peaceful demonstrations but you know these people want violence. There were thirty eight police hurt on the last one, did you know that?"

"And how many demonstrators?"

"The police have to fight back. That's the thing. We have to give the police the power to do their job. We have to nip things in the bud. Get at them before they get at us."

"Jesus, Willie, you're sounding like a fascist. Hitler talked the same way."

"Not at all. This is a peaceful land, threatened by foreign agitators and communist violence. We need to expose them. Need to let them know they cannot enter our streets."

"Frighten them off?"

"Yes. Exactly. Preventive medicine. If they know they will be severely dealt with, no soft touch, they will not enter this green and pleasant land."

"And America will keep on burning peasants in Vietnam."

"That's another matter. It's much more complicated than it might appear."

"No, it's not. But let's get back to you, Willie, what you're doing. You're here to cause trouble?"

"Not exactly." Willie was beginning to look regretful at what he had revealed. "Anyway, it's a means to an end. It's to bring about peace in our country, our green and pleasant land."

"You said that before about the green and pleasant land."

"Peace, anyway."

"Peace in our time?"

"Something like that. Don't forget this is very confidential, Nicholas. And I'm on the same side as you. We all want the Vietnam war to end. But these demonstrations are counter-productive, they just give fuel to the enemy, encourage them in their violence."

Willie was reciting lines he had been taught. Nicholas could not argue. He picked up his cup, took a chair and went to sit with the others.

"What's up?" Hettie asked him quietly. "You've left the fascist on his own. Has he joined the NF or what?"

"I can't tell you. I might later."

"Good. Meanwhile, who is this Millie, then? She seems to think you are very politically compatible, Nicholas. In fact I think you might get your end away tonight, no doubt about that. Is she on the pill?"

"Hettie ! You used to be such a nice girl!"

"That's before I went to work for the BBC. They're all very fresh there, you know. Who is she?"

"She's the daughter of the landowner at home. Every ten years or so, she seduces me."

"Every ten years? So how many times is that so far?"

He laughed. "Perhaps I exaggerate. But she seems very experienced."

"I bet she is. Lively, too, I should think."

"Hettie!"

"Perhaps I should have seduced you years ago. Stopped her getting there first. Ah well, too late now."

Nicholas did not reveal that he had not met Hettie when Millie first seduced him. "I think you're getting over-excited because of the political debate," he told her. "It's what makes girls sleep with socialists, so I've heard. Political debate."

"Is that right? I knew I was missing something. We ought to get back to the demo. What are you reading at the moment?"

"Oh, Trotsky. Mao. Huxley. You know."

"No, you're not. Have you tried Mary Wollstonecraft, though? And Simone de Beauvoir? Essential reading. Come on, we'll talk about that later. Let's get back. What are you doing afterwards? I'm not sure I'll stay for the speeches, Tariq Ali again."

They all stood. By this time the group had grown, swelled by acquaintances and passers by. As they moved down Villiers St to rejoin the march, it was hard to tell where one group ended and another began. A sea of bodies coagulated around the streets, pressing forward, eager to make their mark. The van started moving at last.

"Ho! Ho! Ho Chi Minh!"

"America out! Yanks out! Vietnam for the Vietnamese!"

They shuffled slowly, very slowly, eastwards along the river to Temple; for some reason all demonstrations began in the opposite direction to where they wanted to finish. Then they turned north to Aldwych and up Kingsway to Holborn. Along the way, thousands of others joined in. By the time they swamped Oxford St and deluged Marble Arch, quarter of a million heads could be counted on their way to the speeches in Hyde Park. A detachment, perhaps a few thousand, would take a detour to Grosvenor Square. The U.S. embassy could not be ignored.

Massive demonstrations were cumbersome, predictable and very, very boring. It would take four hours to progress from beginning to end, and the cafes along the route would benefit; only the dedicated and the police stayed with the demo throughout. The police were lined along the ranks of the march, moving steadily in time with them; in addition, pockets of them stood at strategic points en route looking officially good-humoured, as if they had arrived by accident and were not sure what to do. Nicholas engaged the young police-man next to him in a self-conscious debate about the weather. It turned out that he had done a football match the day before, also on overtime as it fell in the middle of his four days off. He was looking forward to one day off on the Monday, then it was back to the grind at West End Central.

"Have you done United this year?"

"I was on duty at Arsenal last season, yeah."

"Two nil! George got two!"

"It was good, yeah. I'm an Arsenal supporter, though."

"Oh, sorry. What about Wembley for the Benfica game, were you working there? I was there. Four two!"

"No, I missed that one."

"Never mind. It's an interesting job you've got."

"Sometimes. When I'm not on demos."

Then the jostle parted them as serries of the crowd pushed forward and found themselves standing beside fresh police. The waiting was endless, the delays were tiring but all the frustration was good-humoured. The chants started again, the demonstrators eager to reach Hyde Park and vent their feelings in full.

"They can't ignore us," Pringle said. "The people have spoken. The workers united will never be defeated. They haven't learned their lesson, have they? They still think their imperialism can control the world, the permanent arms economy will keep capitalism in power. It won't. Capitalism will fall. Vietnam will be liberated."

Nicholas had no answer to that. No doubt Pringle was right, though he seemed to have mixed two or three arguments into one. However, he himself didn't want close involvement in politics. He believed it all, he just didn't want to spend his time doing it. He would rather do something else. Go travelling, perhaps. Afghanistan, India. After the demos were over.

They were close to Hyde Park. Excitement was mounting.

Then a whole swathe of demonstrators, thousands of them, swung left towards Grosvenor Square, the willing carrying the unwilling with them. They were swept away. So were the police guarding them. The ranks of blue were broken apart; the police became part of the battering ram. Nicholas saw Millie disappear beneath the waves. He tried to grab Hettie who was struggling to keep her footing. No-one wanted to fall over, everyone tried to hang on to someone, nobody knew where to go.

The policeman hit him in the face.

It was the same young man whom he had talked football with; he panicked and laid about him. Nicholas could feel the blood running from his nose. He mopped it with his handkerchief, tried to get out of the crush but was helpless. Then he felt himself lifted bodily and carried, feet off the ground, to one side. The crowd swept past.

It was Terry.

"Fuckin' hell, Nick, you want to get out of there, mate. Get yourself duffed up if you hin't careful. Spot of gravy on you already. Still, you'll live."

"God, thanks, Terry. I was worried there. Did you see him? It was that fuzz I was talking to about football, the one who was next to us earlier."

"I saw him. Not a lot we can do about it, though. Time to go I reckon."

"No, I'm going back. I haven't finished. You go. You can't afford to get caught up in it. See you later."

"Right enough." Terry did not hesitate or seek to argue. Having done what was necessary, he wanted to get back to the main demonstration. Nicholas mopped himself up, drew a deep breath, rested for a few minutes and began again, forwards to Grosvenor Square.

"Ho! Ho! Ho Chi Minh!"

"Yanks out! America out!"

"No more napalm!"

Grosvenor Square was a cauldron now, the police barring the way to the embassy, the demonstrators intent on reaching it. Missiles were flying; the crowd were tearing up placards, picking up stones and hurling anything they could find. The police charged, batons whirled. A terrible crack meant that one had landed. The noise was inhuman, a babel of chants and loudspeaker demands and defiance and fear. He looked for the others. They could not have moved much further forward. He saw Pringle, tall and fair haired, twenty yards ahead.

Then the horses came.

Nothing was as terrifying as being charged by police horses. They were huge, strong and highly disciplined. The police riders wielded batons like toys, smashing them on anything below them. They came forwards at a steady trot, insistent, relentless, omitting no-one and showing no mercy. They were going to drive the crowd back and bludgeon everyone in their path.

He saw Willie Dodger.

Willie was on the edge of the pavement. The horses came straight towards him, driving everyone along the road. Willie was taking something out of his pocket, a small bag of some sort. He could get hit at any moment. What was he doing? Nicholas forced his way towards him, sideways along the pavement, away from the main force of the crowd.

Willie put his hand in the bag. Nicholas drew closer and saw a collection of shiny round objects. Willie leaned closer, suicidally close, towards the passing horses.

Marbles.

He was going to roll marbles under the horses' hooves so that the horses fell, chaotically, panic stricken, breaking their legs, unseating their riders, bringing total, brutal havoc.

The police would be at the mercy of the demonstrators they had just been beating back.

Deaths could follow, deaths on both sides, and deaths of horses too. Later the marbles would be found. If necessary Willie would contact the newspapers himself, telling them what to look for. The papers would lead the public backlash against the demonstrators. Killing horses could destroy the whole campaign.

This was the job of an agent provocateur.

"WILLIE! NO!"

He didn't hear.

"STOP IT! WILLIE, STOP IT!"

Willie was crouching down, almost below the horses' rising hooves. Nicholas reached him, bent beside him, stooped, grabbed his shoulder.

Willie struggled for a moment against his own impetus, then overbalanced forwards. He stretched both hands in front of him, tried to regain his balance but was already toppling towards the chaos of animal bodies when a mounted policeman, perhaps unseeing, hit him from the side. With a scream he fell, head foremost, into the melee of horses. He disappeared. No-one saw him there. The horses bucked, whinnied, stumbled backwards and forwards. For a second a space cleared and Willie's head appeared. It was already disfigured, battered from all sides by hooves and legs and bodies, the nose and teeth broken, the eyes closed, the mouth distorted. He was kicked again, then vanished.

A hand pulled Nicholas back.

Terry had not left.

"You come with me."

"Terry - that was Willie - he's under there...."

"You come with me. Nothing you can do'll help him."

"Terry..." He heard a cry come from his own mouth. "Terry!"

"Shut the fuck up! Come with me!"

Terry pulled him away.

"We've got to help him, Terry."

"No, we haven't. I tell you, nothing'll help him, Nick. He's gone. We got to get out of here."

They did.

Thirty-Three

Shoals of rain blew heavily across the woods, almost concealing the farm buildings in the distance. Nicholas turned his back on them and walked away from home. Autumn storms gave no respite, they were cold and raw and insidious. The last of the leaves, always the oak leaves that were last to fall, dropped from the trees and matted the paths underfoot. He pulled his hat further over his head and carried on walking. He wanted to think but he preferred not thinking. He sought a blankness.

Two weeks had passed since Grosvenor Square and much comment had been made. Out of the quarter of a million demonstrators and twenty thousand police, one person had been killed. They said eighty police had been injured. Perhaps they had. They did not count the numbers of demonstrators injured. Only one had been killed. They brought it on themselves. It was bound to happen some time. Determined on violence, showing no respect for the freedom they were granted, abusing their right to demonstrate peaceably, assaulting the police, tragic accidents would happen. Someone was bound to die, sooner or later.

He needed to get away.

In London he could work in a bar, he could be a builder's labourer, he could be a postman. He would not go back to Modern Products in Slough. But he was not going to work at all now. He had enough money to last. He had bought a ticket to Calais. From there, he would hitch a ride as far as it went. Then another one.

Cindy said she was disappointed that he was going away but, to be honest, she did not seem overwhelmed with grief. She just seemed to feel that she might have been consulted.

Millie wanted to join him. He would make very sure that he left quietly. Only his mother would know.

He could write to Hettie. He would see Pringle when he got back. Terry would be away but might be on leave at Christmas.

He should be home by then. Whatever Christmas would be like in another country, he could not spend it without Helena or without Bill. Perhaps they would be fine. He was buggered, though, if he was going to put it to the test. Helena would find a man to share Christmas with, Bill would find another companion to feed the cattle. The thought almost made him cry in the rain.

He did not want to think about this or anything else.

He had never wanted to travel before. Now he wanted the first truck, or car, or motor bike heading out of Calais. Heading east, heading south, heading for the alternatives.

He turned back towards home.

269

"Well, bless my soul!" Mr Goodbody said. "Bless my ruddy soul, look at that!"

"Body!"

"Sorry, mother. But just look at that!"

On television, an army of spectators at the test match was helping the ground staff to clear the outfield of puddles. At lunchtime, on the last day at the Oval, late in August, a thunderstorm had swept the field, preventing England's long-awaited victory. A thunderstorm had also halted Bill's harvest and they had all gone home to watch the match. Nicholas took his sandwiches to eat them with Mr Goodbody. The sun came out again at the Oval at two fifteen. All afternoon the mopping up ran on. At four forty five play resumed. The nation watched. Australia still had five wickets left. Jarman and Inverarity were at the crease. Surely England couldn't get them out by close of play?

"Come you on together!" Mr Goodbody was a quiet man in his old age. As he often said, he was over eighty now and couldn't afford to get excited. Today was different, though. He was frantically chewing biscuits, cleaning his glasses and shifting restlessly in his chair. The commentators were talking about the wicket taking spin.

"Just you stop talking that load of old squit!" he shouted at them. "Get on with it!"

"Body!"

"Sorry, mother."

"Nicholas, you calm him down. He's blooming hopeless. Be doing himself a mischief do he aren't careful."

"I'll do my best, Mrs Goodbody. But it is very exciting."

"You're as bad as him."

England could not get a wicket. Cowdrey, the captain, tried everything to dislodge the two entrenched Australians. The wicket was dead. He turned to D'Oliveira. As so often, the old warhorse produced the goods. A beautiful off cutter inveigled its way through Jarman's defence and took the off bail.

"He's out! That's one less! Four to go!"

But only thirty five minutes were left.

Cowdrey promptly removed D'Oliveira and brought back Underwood. The sun was out and the pitch was drying rapidly. Underwood suddenly became unplayable.

"He's gone!" exclaimed Mr Goodbody. "He's caught out!" Mallett was caught by Brown.

"He's out again!" he meant to say that a new batsman, McKenzie, was out too, but the occasion was too much for him. Underwood had taken two wickets in one over, both caught by Brown in the leg trap.

"Two more to go," Nicholas said.

Gleeson stayed for twelve minutes. Mr Goodbody ate three more biscuits. Nicholas sipped his tea. Mrs Goodbody did her knitting. Complete silence reigned.

"He's bowled him!" the two men cried in unison. Mrs Goodbody nearly leaped from her chair in shock as Gleeson's off stump was knocked back.

Then Inverarity faced Underwood. The other batsman, Connolly, was not a batsman at all, but Inverarity had battled for four hours and seemed ready to bat for forty four if necessary. But it wasn't necessary, there were only a few minutes to go. Somehow England had to get Inverarity down the other end and let Underwood get at Connolly.

Underwood bowled to Inverarity. No-one was optimistic. Inverarity played no shot.

"He's let it go. He hasn't played a shot. They're appealing!"

"He's out!"

Inverarity, imperturbable intellectual of the Australian team, had suffered a brainstorm. He had left a perfectly straight ball and was given out lbw by umpire Charlie Elliott.

"We've won!"

"I don't believe it! We've won!"

"Calm down, Body, else you'll get one of them turns."

"It's like '26 all over again. And '53."

"We watched it here in '53, Mr Goodbody, didn't we?"

"And we'd have watched it in '26, given half a chance."

"Except I wasn't born and TV wasn't invented."

"Except for that. Well, the hell if I know."

"Body!"

"Well, mother, it don't come round too often. I likely swore in '26 an' all."

"You never used to swear in them days. I blame Hitler. It was them land army girls started it."

"Course, we still hin't won the Ashes, Nicholas, hiv we?"

"No, Mr Goodbody. The series is a draw so they keep the Ashes. We deserved to win it, though. It was only rain stopped us in the other matches."

"Bless my soul. You got another brew going, mother?"

"If you don't do any more of that swearing. You needn't expect any more tea when you're swearing like a German."

"Sorry, mother." She went out and Mr Goodbody and Nicholas looked at each other and laughed. "What a day, eh?"

About the author

Jeremy Cameron (1947-2023) was a writer, walker, probation officer, sportsman, and Union official. He was born in Norfolk, and returned to his beloved West Acre upon his retirement from the Probation Service in Walthamstow, North East London.

He is best known for his crime fiction books, including *It Was An Accident*, the second book in the Nicky Burkett series, which was adapted into a film starring Chiwetel Ejiofor and Thandiwe Newton.

Throughout his life, Jeremy embarked on some very, very long walks. Most notable in recent years was his walk (at the age of 62 and suffering from a heart condition) from Hook of Holland to Istanbul, which he wrote about in *Never Again*. In his words, never again would he "do anything quite so stupid." After which he set off to walk around all the places in England beginning with the letter Q.

Jeremy died in 2023 – it was an accident.

Praise for the Nicky Burkett series:

Vinnie Got Blown Away

'This is a short sharp shock of a novel. Cameron renders the speech of disaffected London youth better than anyone else.'

GQ

'Like some distant, downbeat relative of Anthony Burgess's A Clockwork Orange, Jeremy Cameron's earthily gripping debut thriller is a fast, funny trawl through the territory of London's new outlaw underclass ... a masterly piece of storytelling.'

Financial Times

It Was An Accident

'A wonderful thriller ... an absolute cracker, the superb narrative voice, North East London streetspeak, is so convincingly done that it makes the residents of Albert Square sound like Dick Van Dyke in Mary Poppins.'

The Independent

Brown Bread in Wengen

'Warm, engaging and shot through with genuine humanity.'
Probation Journal

Hell on Hoe Street

'Consistently entertaining and funny ... a real east meets west roller-coaster.'
The Times

ALSO BY JEREMY CAMERON

Fiction

The Nicky Burkett Series

- Vinnie Got Blown Away

- It Was An Accident

- Hell on Hoe Street

- Brown Bread in Wengen

- Wider Than Walthamstow

For Teenagers

- Teenage Kicks

Non-Fiction

Travel Writing

- Never Again: A walk from Hook of Holland to Istanbul

- Quite Quintessential: A walk around Britain to all the places beginning with 'Q'.

Tennis and Cricket

- How To Be President (of the Norfolk Lawn Tennis Association)

- Life Begins

- A Season in West Norfolk

The Probation Service

- Tales from the Probation Service

ACKNOWLEDGEMENTS

With thanks to Veronica Stallwood for providing her editorial comments on the draft manuscript.

BV - #0087 - 170424 - C0 - 197/132/16 - PB - 9781739232429 - Gloss Lamination